Peter Pan
Betwixt-and-Between

Peter Von Brown

Second Edition

Text Copyright © 2013 by Peter Von Brown

Cover Design & Artwork Copyright © 2013 by Peter Von Brown

All rights reserved.

#PPBaB

petervonbrown.com

This book is a work of fiction.

References to real locales, historical events or people are used fictitiously. Places, incidents, names and characters are products of imagination and any resemblance to actual locales, events or persons, living or dead, is entirely coincidental. No part of this book may be used or reproduced without written permission, except in the case of articles or reviews embodying brief passages in quotations.

ISBN: 978-1468027075

FOR ANON
WHO MADE IT A JOY TO EXPLORE BARRIE'S PAN ONCE MORE

ACKNOWLEDGEMENTS

This novel most likely would have never come to light without the encouragement and reaction from two individuals. They more than reignited my passion for this tale, as their enthusiasm and suggestions shaped and refined it into a better story overall. From the bottom of my inkwell, a wealth of gratitude to my #1 fan, Anon, and to Andrea Jones, author of the *Hook & Jill* Saga. I must also give credit to Sunshine for so quickly bringing the word "telluric" to my attention when I'd been bogged down with over-thinking the issue. Certainly not least, my editors for their tweaks.

A SPECIAL THANK YOU TO SIR JAMES MATTHEW BARRIE

FOREWORD

While writing *Peter Pan's NeverWorld*, I grappled with another story. Rather a lack of a story. There's a gap in Barrie's tales of Peter Pan. But NeverWorld had to be tamed, so I looked away from the void.

I never truly left it alone.

How could I not muse on the time separating *Peter Pan in Kensington Gardens* and *Peter and Wendy*? Given the parallels between them, clearly Barrie changed his scope of the character. A fine answer, if only the latter didn't refer back to the former as having happened!

The long and short of it: How did a wild, eternal infant in a London park become the Boy Who Wouldn't Grow Up fighting pirates in the Neverland? Which, of course, requires growing up — and ceasing again? Tall questions for such a small boy.

Many years later while rereading *The Little White Bird* (the novel which contains the Kensington Gardens story) a bit of Barrie leapt out at me. I wondered what would happen if I took the Narrator at face value at that bit. Suddenly the story bridge framework spanned ahead. One idea locked into another and solved the next. I began writing, having worked halfway through when the window closed on Peter Pan works. My pen went down.

When I found myself in the realm again, I revisited the book. I tinkered with other avenues from Barrie, threw out characters and performed other literary rites. I dove back into London and the Neverland.

Along with appreciation and respect, I approached this novel in the same fashion as *Peter Pan's NeverWorld*: incorporating Barrie's own writings and ideas, maintaining accordance with what he'd established and upholding his style.

For those expecting Tinker Bell, alas, it is not to be. Pan's first encounter with Tink deserves its own tale, not crammed into an already awfully big adventure. Other known characters whisper through the pages; some appear. My novel does not span the entire gap of the two Barrie books. It's the story of how a baby came to be the boy of the magical island.

I present the lost years of Peter Pan.

Peter Von Brown

Contents

Chapter 1	Questioning	1
Chapter 2	Changes	16
Chapter 3	Alternatives	34
Chapter 4	Understanding	51
Chapter 5	Lessons	76
Chapter 6	Huitzili	100
Chapter 7	Flight	111
Chapter 8	Meetings	122
Chapter 9	Adventure!	135
Chapter 10	Discoveries	166
Chapter 11	Misgivings	180
Chapter 12	Plans	196
Chapter 13	Execution	214
Chapter 14	Forever	225

Chapter 1
Questioning

One night, of all nights, it happened.

Peter Pan lay in the grass amid the trees of Bird Island, an infant kicking his legs gaily, looking up at the many stars and wondering. The stars winked back occasionally, making Peter even more good-spirited. He thought for sure they could hear his thoughts and often he would think things out to them. He never did get a reply other than friendly winks and when Peter caught forty of them, he fell asleep. He normally slept during the day, so that he could have his reign of the Gardens during Lock-out Time. Perhaps due to the irregularity of it, this night nap produced a troubling dream, the first of many throughout Pan's life.

At first the dream went pleasantly wherein he left his Thrush's Nest boat and took to the air delighting in his power of flight restored. He zipped around the Kensington Gardens, happily sailing in the sky without a care. So much did he enjoy his aerial maneuvers and devil-may-care journey that he took no heed of where he flew. So not long after, unfamiliar territory stretched around him. He heard crying. He assumed it to be his own and took to crying himself. After a bit, though, he noticed that some of his sobs did not match up with the others. He quieted himself. After a few leftover gasps, he listened intently to the weeping in the distance. The gasps from this weeping became more frequent. Eventually, these gasps turned into sharp little quips of sound.

Peter Pan hovered in midair, unable to move from curiosity. He could not figure from which direction the strange cries came. He kept listening and before he could tell that a switch had been made, the sound turned to a sharp laughter. The laughter surged through him and gave him a chill like the very first night he spent in Kensington Gardens after his triumphant escape from the nursery. He did not like the feeling even one little bit and wished, for the first time in too long, that his mother could have comforted him. Thinking of his mother within the dream while the boyish laughter still cackled must have been too much to bear and he awoke with a jolt.

His goat bleated next to him, nudging him. The bleats echoed the sobs in the dream. Though it proved a tricky task, Peter put it out of his mind except for the part about flying. Aside from his strict duty to assist children who pass on, he had not been really flying since his eventful trip back to his nursery. It would be so sweet to fly around again, he thought. But then he wondered where. Certainly he had no reason to go elsewhere. He had such a good life here among the birds, animals and fairies in the Kensington Gardens, playing all the time.

The goat had not awoken him without purpose. The time had come for his nightly trip around the Gardens searching for children who may have gotten left behind after Lock-out. He pushed himself up and climbed onto the goat's back to begin the rounds.

He gaily pranced around with the goat. But once again, it seemed that he would be alone with the regular night-time inhabitants. No children to be found. In the distance, the lights surrounding the newest Little House went out; or rather the fairies left the scene, satisfied with their work for the night.

Peter sighed that yet another Little House would disappear come morning with no one to have reveled in its beauty, waking literally to the magic that surrounded him always. Since that first time when Maimie Mannering found herself in the fairies' lodging, he could remember only perhaps a handful that had done the same. Each one of the visitors after Lock-out had been a girl. Yet none of them so memorable as Maimie. In fact, if anything extraordinary had ever happened with their visits, he could not in the least recall. Peter knew it to have been too terribly long ago that anyone spent the night.

Feeling ponderous again, he now wondered why no little boys got stuck overnight in the Gardens. Still obsessed with behaving like a real boy, he so wanted to play with one ever since Walter Stephen Matthews left, who had already met a tragic end even before Peter had a chance to say hello. Unless traveling part of the way with him to the other place counts. But for Peter it did not mean much. He never got to spend time with Walter. Just his little grave remained. And he never found any others. And that all happened more or less a whole year ago.

Suddenly he heard whimpering, perhaps even crying. He kicked the goat gently as one would a horse and dashed off to the source of the sound. Down through the Flower Walk path they went, ignoring fairies and leaping over the gates of the iron black fence lining the Gardens. But the closer Peter and the goat approached, the softer the whimpers became. He urged the goat to go faster but to no avail. By the time Peter Pan found the little whimpering child no more sounds came at all. Peter leapt off the goat. He kneeled down next to the figure. He tapped the child to make sure. He had his hopes — but alas — he would not escort this one to the Little House the fairies made that night. Instead his duty fell to serving as escort to the other place. Then he saw. A boy! Here had been his chance and he did not come in time to save him! Peter sat with tears rolling down his cheeks for a whole minute before he mustered up the gumption to complete his task. He wiped away his tears and reached for his pipes. He began to play a tune he felt that he had played one too many times. This melancholy melody always had the same result. Anyone strolling by the Gardens at this time would have heard what might have been the whistling of the wind, or perhaps the splash of moonlight into the Serpentine.

Peter Pan kept up his music, waiting for the spirit of the little boy to blow out along with the wind

5

Peter Pan kept up his music, waiting for the spirit of the little boy to blow out along with the wind that he played and show up in the moonlight he summoned. He shut his eyes tight when he made his sweet natural music, except for the occasional peek. Soon he saw a spark that would have been in the young lad's eye and he drew his music to a close. "Oh," said the boy, "I say, am I dead?"

Hearing it from the boy struck a chord in Peter much deeper than if Pan had to tell the boy. "Yes," he said. "My name is Peter Pan. I will take you part of the way so that you shall not be scared."

"Are you not to go with me all the way?"

Peter felt the tingling as his own spirit wrestled to get out. "No, I am not able to do that. But O! How I wish that I could. I should rather like it if you could stay here with me."

"Then I shall. I'm pleased to meet you. My name is Jake Mortimer Higgins."

For a moment or three longer than he really should have, Peter entertained the notion of allowing Jake to remain with him in the Gardens. How nice it would have been, to have a real boy (ethereal though he might be) with whom to play at hoops, and jump the gates of park pathways and play hide-and-seek. What fun to know a real friend to talk to each night other than the birds and the meddlesome fairies. But finally he shook his head no. That went against the rules. "Solomon Caw would not allow it. Nor the fairies."

"Solomon Caw? I feel as if I know him," said Jake, ignoring Peter's naysay.

"Solomon is in charge of Bird Island. He fulfills the requests –"

"Ah, yes," interrupted Jake. "I remember now. I should like to see old Solomon again! How is he holding up?"

Peter nearly answered when he heard a sloshing of water. Both he and Jake turned to look. Peter could not be fully sure of what he saw for he had never seen anything like it. If asked he would only have been able to say a grey streak coupled with a splashy plopping. If he thought further, he would have remarked that the scene wavered like looking through rippling water. Or, if he had any knowledge of such a thing, he would have said he observed the event as if looking through frosted glass. He could not even be sure of it being a person or whirlpool. But one thing did strike him with certainty. Jake Higgins had gone with it!

Peter looked around and not even the body of his new friend lay in front of him. He could see only the usual sight of fairies skipping about the Gardens and his goat grazing in the distance.

7

"Jake!" he shouted. "Jake!" No response, except a few fairies turned to look his way. He wanted to know what happened. Had he ever really been talking to Jake at all? Then an idea of what must have happened struck him. He pulled out his pipes and played the Fairy Reveille. Not that a tune by that name truly existed. It refers to a tune of which Peter had become rather fond to stir up the wee folk and although it never followed the same arrangement of notes as the last hearing, it had always been one of the tunes that the fairies could not resist. Some of the fey folk gathered and when Peter spied them dancing, he stopped playing.

A gentleman fairy harrumphed and others gazed at Peter with an undancey gaze.

"Pray continue!" a fairy lady asked sweetly.

"I want to know which one of you fairies did mischief to Jake!" demanded Peter.

The gentleman fairy replied, "You're making no sense." Even though they knew quite well that they would have done the mischief if given the chance, the fairies became incensed that Peter would accuse them. They started to scatter.

"Don't leave!" Peter wailed.

The lady fairy flew up to Peter's eyes. She looked into them and saw that the boy felt sincerely hurt. She thought for a moment and then asked, "Is this Jake that little human boy here moments ago?"

Peter sniffed and at the same time his eyes lit up. "Yes!"

"I watched from over yonder," she said.

"So tell me," said Peter, crossing his little arms, "which one of you mischiefed him?"

"Dear Peter Pan," she said as if rehearsed, "no fairy mischief took place. I can assure you on penalty of the Queen's wrath. In fact, fairies had nothing to do with it at all!"

"Then who did?" Peter plopped down to the ground, chubby little legs crossed.

"I can only tell you that I have seen it before."

"You have?" asked Peter with both delight and terror.

"As sure as my wings. Alas, what I cannot tell you is anything about it. I doubt many fairies can. We just don't fiddle with that blurry grey."

"None of you fairy folk knows what it is?"

"Perhaps some do. Not many of us care, so long as the effect is getting rid of the humans prowling around the Gardens after Lock-out."

Her response annoyed Peter a bit, but he did not become angry, for despite himself, he could see it from their point of view. "Very well," said Peter. "I shall go see the only one who might be able to tell me." With that, Peter called his goat and rode to the tree where he would find wise old Solomon Caw.

In a flurry of frantic words, Peter Pan explained the events of the evening. He took no heed of Solomon's stocking, now so full that it barely had any room left.

After rustling his feathers for some time and letting out a cough, Solomon Caw responded. "The fairy is correct. It happens more than you know."

"Even though I patrol the Gardens looking for children I never noticed? Bah!"

"Well, it rarely ever happens here. You got lucky in reaching the boy just this once."

"*The* boy? Is it always Jake?"

Solomon cawed in laughter but saw it to be no joking matter for Peter Pan so he stopped cawkling immediately. "No, no. It is always a different boy."

"And am I not able to keep one?"

"No on this notion as well. You are not the one who keeps them."

"Who does?" Peter asked, leaning forward.

"That is too much for a Betwixt-and-Between to find out about." Solomon coughed as if in punctuation.

"Please tell me. I so want to have a playmate!"

"I'm afraid you left that option behind long ago."

"I didn't know," said Peter weakly.

"That's too bad that you did not know," Solomon said compassionately.

"You should have told me!"

Solomon looked sidelong at the baby boy. "Should I have?"

Peter opened his mouth to speak, but he saw impatience in the rapidly moving eye of the wise old crow and it made him most uneasy.

"Now, if you'll excuse me," Solomon said with another cough, "I have plenty to do." The crow flapped higher into the tree.

Dejected to leave with so little, Peter went to a particular tree, in which he had taken up residence when he slept during the day (much to the dismay of a disgruntled and displaced chipmunk who now ekes out a living on the far end of the island trading good moss for bits of candy with the birds) and curled up inside it for the remainder of the night. He thought intensely, preoccupied with what Solomon spoke of, curious as to what happened to Jake, or for that matter, all the boys. He thought himself to sleep and did not reawaken until just before Lock-out the next night. He decided that he must make his rounds of the Gardens sooner in hopes of not being too late for the children. The instant the bell clang signaled the Closing of the Gates, he called to his goat and began the hunt. But he encountered nothing that night. So he spent the rest of the night in the place where he met Jake and pretended to play with him.

He tried this new routine each night thereafter. But he soon came to try with desperate hopes, for not until moons later did something of importance happen again. Peter Pan had the unfortunate duty to accompany a little girl to the other place. She did not have the least inclination to stay, despite Peter's attempts at engaging her in conversation. He had questioned her about Jake Higgins, but she just shrugged. When they had gotten about halfway, the little miss turned to Peter Pan.

"Thank you ever so much, but I can go the rest of the way myself." She waved goodbye.

Peter Pan watched her go and his heart filled with sadness. He sighed deeply, and then turned back. He went back toward his little sleep-like body in the Gardens. As he prepared to reconnect with himself, he heard that same sploshy noise and caught a grey glimpse!

'No!' thought Peter Pan.

He dove back into himself. "No! No! No! I won't have it!" he shouted.

He ran off without his goat to complain to Solomon Caw. He found the old crow lying down as if in rest, but Peter Pan did not care. He would be heard.

"It happened again! The very same thing!"

"You cannot stop it from happening."

"It isn't fair!" Peter yelled and his little eyes narrowed.

"Calm down."

"No! It's not fair! It's not fair! It's not fair! I never get to play with any of them!"

"You've played with one or two children before."

"But they always leave! They fear to stay with me!"

"You belong here. They do not."

"I can't even go the whole way with those that die!"

"Yes," coughed Caw. "That's true."

"But I don't want that to be true!"

"As you belong here, they belong there. It's the way –"

"No! It's not the way I want it!"

"Calm yourself, little Betwixt-and-Between."

"Don't call me that!"

Solomon coughed. "It's what you are."

"I don't want to be that anymore! I don't want any of this anymore! I don't want to know children for a short time only! I want one to stay with me!"

"I cannot help you," replied Caw to his rant.

"Then I won't help *you*!"

"Whatever do you mean?"

"I'm not taking any more children to forever away."

"But –"

"I won't!" Peter folded his wee little arms.

"But you took on that responsibility. It is not good form to shun it."

"Well, I shall."

"Long ago you promised to do it. It is your duty. You *must* respect that." A cough.

"How dare you tell me what I must do!" yelled Peter. "That's why I ran away in the first place, isn't it?" he snipped.

"You didn't want to grow up. That's why you ran away."

"Growing up means giving up games! How dare my parents speak of what I would be when I became a man! And how dare *you,* Solomon Caw!"

For the first time, the crow raised his voice at baby Pan. "I tell you again: BAD FORM!"

"I don't care!"

"I do not deserve such treatment. We here in the Gardens have been very kind to you. We birds and fairies did not have to take you in."

"Maybe you shouldn't have."

"Mayhap not," spat the crow.

"Maybe I don't belong here."

"Mayhap not," the old bird said again. "But so long as you are here, you will –"

"I will *not*! I never want to do it again! You cannot make me!" Peter started to cry.

Solomon sighed. "Indeed. But if this is truly your decision, then do not expect things to be the same."

Peter ignored the comment, but he should not have. He scampered away in a huff, leaving Solomon Caw to his much needed rest.

Chapter 2
Changes

For the next few days, Peter Pan could not quell his churning feelings. He made himself miserable when he thought how he would never have any lasting human friends. He felt terrible that he had yelled at Solomon. But he meant what he said and would not apologize for it. The thought that little children should perish and not know the way! Sometimes he felt guilty for abandoning them. But he knew they would abandon him, so anger quickly turned to spite which in turn made him realize no one would to stay with him if he remained such unappealing company. He did make one attempt, mostly from force of habit. He thought he could make amends by guiding the girl. But as he neared, he pulled his ghost-like self back, for he saw she could do very well on her own without him.

He thought how Solomon had nearly kicked him out of the Gardens. Perhaps going away would be best after all, he would sometimes think. But then that same problem presented itself: Where on earth would he go? And how would he get there? Sometimes the sadness of it all overwhelmed him. He had stopped his nightly rounds altogether, even the carefree skipping about. Instead he just reflected in his tree. When he brought out his pipes, he played morose songs that might have caused flowers to wilt. Often he lay on his back, looking at the stars. If he were not able to talk to them as he did, he might have gone crazy with anguish. His goat sensed his uneasiness, but its attempts to cheer him may as well never have occurred. Eventually the goat kept its distance.

Some time after his tantrum, Peter Pan became the loneliest he could ever remember. He peered out from his hollow tree and could hear the birds arguing over who took the best piece of string and whether or not rain hindered nest making. He then figured he could at least play with the fairies. They must have been quite depressed themselves without any cheery tunes for their parties.

So the little Betwixt-and-Between ventured forth from his hollow tree. To his surprise, it proved very difficult to climb out. His hips scraped the sides like never before. After he pried himself loose, he examined the hole but found that it did not look any different. He skipped away, but very soon discovered that he still had no mind for such jocularity. He walked slowly onward instead. As he went, he noticed that little animals like ducks and squirrels darted away from him. Two rabbits stared, twitching their noses. But in the end, as Pan approached, they ran away too. Normally he could have run amok with them, petting and tickling and chasing. Peter assumed his sour countenance to be the cause of their strange behavior. He let them scurry without a chase, for he came out to entertain himself with the fairies.

As their lights always gave them away, locating a throng of them proved easy. Luckily tonight happened to be one of their affairs. If the merriment were not enough to let him know, he also found one of the invitation-cards on the ground. He read through all of the particulars and noted that next to the usual "P.P." in the corner he saw a question mark. Wondering if he'd show, were they? Peter meandered over to the gathering, his pipes ready in hand.

Upon seeing the boy coming, the fairies applauded and cheered. Quite pleased, Peter sat down in the grass next to the party. He tasted a few of their feast items, having only eaten scraps of bread left outside his tree by some kind birds. Even though so little, the food satisfied him and for a time he did not feel so bad. Sooner than later, some of the fairies climbed on the table and licked at the sugar from some of the delicious pastries, still others mashed the root butter into the table-cloth, while some nasty ones hurled breads at each other. The party having gotten quite indelicate, Queen Mab ordered it swept away, all too eager for Peter Pan's pipes. He played yet another fairy favorite.

It felt just like it always had and Peter managed to forget all about his troubles. This particular party lost sight of its original reason to celebrate, whatever it might have been, because it soon became a celebration of Peter's return. The revelry stretched on much longer than usual and Peter Pan did not get to see the end of it. He had been dancing around rather wildly himself, making up for lost time. As a result, he tuckered out quickly. He had not even known that he went to sleep right there in the grass near the Baby's Palace.

When the festivities finally drew to a close, the fairies found themselves with an immovable Peter Pan. None of them succeeded in trying to wake him and none of them wanted to perform any transformational magic on him lest they forget and leave him that way by mistake. After more attempts at rousing him, the Queen finally decided to paint him the color of night like fairy houses. That way they would be able to see him, but the humans strolling in the park that day would not.

The next evening, little Peter Pan finally woke. He had slept so deeply that day that not even the hustle and bustle of the Garden visitors stirred him. If it were not for troubling dreams which he took for some sort of reality, he would have been in a good mood considering the fun of late. But he had no idea that he had even been sleeping, nor that he'd been painted. Nighttime had come again as it is wont to do since it always has to share in half the fun of the clock, and the spell wore off. He wondered what happened to the lovely party. He felt embittered and upset again. Actually, if he had known of Queen Mab's ability to paint him the color of night, he would have requested it all too often. He would then be able, of course, to roam around the Gardens during the day. But he had no idea and the fairies preferred it that way to be sure.

He looked all around, but strangely enough, no fairies were about. Since Peter had the impression of it being still the same night, he went to his tree and crawled inside to go to bed. Once again, he marveled at what a tight squeeze it had somehow become. He ran his hand along the edge of the hole, but it seemed just the same. He did not know he had slept all day so he concluded that the morning would be coming soon and though he had so much sleep he decided it time for bed and fell asleep yet again. Even more troubling dreams filled his head this time. The foreboding laughter and sorrow of his dreams kept waking him. Jake showed up in them. But always he could not save him. Peter Pan hoped that Jake had found grace. The little confused lad tossed and turned all day.

Finally he heard the clanging of the Closing of the Gate and made the increasingly difficult effort to get out of the tree. He thought of nothing but taking a leisurely sail in his boat. He'd leave the other side of the Gardens alone and just have a float. He walked across Bird Island toward the Serpentine. A few fairies were already out and about on the island. As Peter passed them they gave him funny looks, aiming their gaze at his head. He gave them funny looks in return; trying to keep up with what he assumed to be a new game on their part. If he could have heard their whisperings to each other, he would have known they remarked on how much more hair Peter had.

The walk seemed shorter than usual and soon Peter stood next to his Thrush Nest boat. He reached for the shovel he used as his oar and then gingerly sat inside. How strange, thought Peter, that there didn't seem to be much room. Perhaps he sat in the boat differently from his usual way. He shifted his position but in the process nearly capsized. He moved back to how he sat originally but tucked his legs in underneath himself. Although he should have, he made no connection between this and the tree-hole. Too eager to take a ride, he decided not to think about the boat.

Gliding along the Serpentine, all his troubles seemed to be floating away in the ripples behind. He relaxed in the moment, enjoying the serenity of the ride. He did not even look - from shore to shore. He stopped paddling, laying the shovel down inside the boat. Then he cautiously moved so as to lie down. His feet hung over the edge of the Nest. He drifted like this for some time, staring up at the stars. He did not speak to them so as not to rekindle any unpleasant thoughts.

He drifted like this for some time, staring up at the stars.

Night-time in Kensington Gardens happened around him and he gave no care at all. So long as he could float along the lake, he could forget it all. As can be imagined, he also forgot all about the time. He didn't fall asleep, but he did fall into the calming reflectiveness of the water. He felt as if he were neither here nor there. Neither then nor now. In fact, it felt very much like when he would wrestle out his own spirit to journey with children to the other place. The hours wore on with Peter adrift.

A sudden bump roused Peter Pan. At first he did not know what had happened. He sat up and peered around. It became apparent rather quickly. The boat had made its way to the shore. He climbed out of the boat, thinking to have a leisurely stroll around the Gardens. He spied some fairies having a game of limbo using the stem of a tulip. (Not many know that the fairies first played this challenging activity long before the humans caught wind of it.) A naughty child must have picked the tulip only to discard it, so the fairies thought some use should come of it. Later they would fashion the petals into a hat, vest and skirt. When Peter Pan approached, he saw their little heads turn. But instead of cheers that he could come and play the pipes, something else happened. Their wee eyes grew very large and some of the fairies gasped. They all skittered off in an array of directions so quickly that the tulip stem limbo bar did not hit the ground until after they had all gone.

Their behavior annoyed Peter Pan, but he knew he could only blame himself. After all, hadn't he been ignoring the fairies in favor of melancholy? He went to grab a rabbit but it, too, ran off. Peter sighed. He tried to play as he had before all this happened, but he could only think of Jake each time he thought he played like a real boy.

Dread still weighing upon him, Peter went back to the boat, squoze in and paddled to the other side. He trudged back to his tree and entered. Or rather he tried to enter. It seemed that he could not fit this time. He stomped his feet and tried again. But each way he went in — head first, feet first, arm first, side first — made little matter. He could not get in at all! He kicked the tree and plopped himself down. He rubbed his foot. Once soothed, he resigned himself to sleeping curled up next to the tree.

He lay unaware of fairies watching from afar. Once absolutely certain that the now bigger Peter Pan slept, they flew off to see Queen Mab. They requested to see her due to a great emergency. At first she refused audience for she happened to be in the middle of her nectar bath. But Colandrion, the courtier, insisted, telling the attendant something rather fearful. The attendant shuddered and darted off to tell the Queen.

The news startled the Queen so much her tub tipped over and she did not even remark on the dirty water seeping all over her clean chamber floor. She shook herself dry, put on her simplest (yet still elegant) robe and walked out to the group. She hoped the attendant exaggerated, for outright exposure of Peter Pan and fairies could not be taken lightly at all.

When she entered the chamber, the fairies bowed and greeted her in the usual way. But she stopped the formalities. "Forego the pleasantries and talk of the matter forthwith." Each of them spoke, sometimes at once, giving their piece and interrupting each other, but they managed to relate the event in whole. It sounded even more awful with the details.

"Oh dear!" she said. "Oh dear Oh dear Oh dear," she repeated as she flew off toward the sleeping Peter Pan. She found him slumbering just as the fairies had said, curled up with a leg arched. She said a few nasty things not loud enough for the boy to hear. Then she exhaled noisily and threw the magic over him like pulling up the covers so that once more he became the color of night. She shook her head and flew off, her mind now occupied only with the growing problem. She returned immediately to her chamber, where Colandrion and the others awaited. She spoke of what must be done. And soon.

As it will, the spell had worn off when Peter awoke the next night. Very shortly after getting up, he thought he heard crying. Instinctively he motioned to summon his goat, but very quickly he remembered. He did not do that anymore. The child would just leave anyway. He thought maybe, just perhaps, he could still travel along. So he began to wrestle out his spirit. But nothing happened. Maybe he did it wrong. He tried again. Alas he could not do it. Before it had been as easy as standing up, but now it seemed like he had never done it and did not know how.

Frustrated, he decided to find his goat and go for a ride. Not to find the child, he convinced himself, but just for a ride. So he summoned the goat with a tune like a cheery bleating and the goat happily pranced right over. But when Peter mounted the goat, it bleated unhappily. It buckled at the knees. Despite Peter's kick command, the goat did not go forward. Peter verbally commanded the goat. But still it did not budge. Its bleats sounded pained, angry even. Finally it shook violently. Peter toppled off the goat and whumped to the ground. The goat trotted off without him. How strange, Peter thought, since he knew himself to be very light.

If Peter Pan felt very upset before, he reached twice as upset as that now. It seemed that every creature in Kensington Gardens shunned him and he wanted to know why. It brought to mind the fateful night when he had re-entered the Gardens by flying back without realizing he'd not been a bird. Just as the fairies and animals had then, they all now ran from him, so he could hardly ask any of them. He knew of only one he could ask, but he found himself reluctant to go back. He predicted the scene in his mind and felt ever so glum when he could not imagine himself coming out on top in the conversation. He sailed back to the island.

Soon he stood under the branch, but a bare branch. Solomon Caw usually did his figures from this very branch at this very time. Pan looked up at the rest of the tree, walked around it and stood back to examine it further. But he did not see the wise old crow. He nearly took this to mean that he should go away. But nowhere in the Gardens did he seem to be welcome. So he resigned himself to sit beneath the tree and await Solomon's return. He sat and sat, using the time to think about what he might say to the old bird. He decided to pretend the previous argument had never happened at all. While he thought, he watched some clouds that could still be seen against the twilight sky drift by until they had drifted the whole way across the tree. Then he heard a cough. He turned sharply to have another look. From this vantage point he could see a rustle of wing in the shadows.

"Solomon Caw?" he asked.

Another cough responded.

"Where have you been?" the boy asked.

"I've been here all along, Peter Pan."

"Why did you not say anything?"

"Why didn't *you!*"

Peter did not like his tone.

Solomon spoke again. "So, what have you been up to since declaring yourself free of your chore?"

How nice to not have to do his chore! But hadn't he been miserable with his freedom? "I've been doing all the things I normally do, except…"

A cough. "Tell me what is on your mind, Peter Pan." The old crow already knew, certainly, but he wanted the boy to say it for himself.

Peter Pan did not know where to begin. He had the feeling that he had failed at controlling the conversation. Another passing cloud filled the time while he tried to think of how to ask what he came to ask.

But Solomon waited no more and spoke for him. "You want to know why fairies now flee, why the birds and animals scurry away, why your tree and boat shrank, why you cannot wrestle out your spirit and why you're so tired all the time."

Peter's eyes widened. He looked up, but shadows still hid Solomon. "That's more than exactly right! How did you know?"

"Come now, Pan, did you think I would not know?"

Surely a bird must have tipped him off at the very least thought Peter. "But…do you have…an answer for me?"

Solomon cleared his throat into a rather pronounced cough. "Of course I have."

Peter waited for the answer. But Caw remained silent.

The boy could not fathom why he delayed. "Will you not tell me?"

"I will. But you will not like what I say."

Already Peter did not like what he had said. How much worse could it get? "I am ready to hear it," Peter said, trying to sound unafraid.

"There is fear in your voice."

"And there is a scratchiness in yours," Peter snapped, for indeed, Caw sounded tired.

"You know the thing you had hoped wouldn't happen?" Solomon said snidely. "Well, I'm afraid it *is* happening."

Peter still did not understand him, looking quizzically up to the dark patches of shadow in the tree leaves.

"You will know by looking at yourself, Peter Pan."

"Kindly stop speaking in riddles," the boy requested.

"Go and see for yourself in the Serpentine. Peer over into the water. You will see."

"But what if I don't see?"

"You will."

"What if I don't understand?"

"If you want," replied the crow, "you may return here and I can answer any further questions without any riddles."

"But –"

"Go on."

As with the rest of the conversation, Peter did not like this one bit. But he figured that he better do as the old crow said if it would get to the bottom of things. So he pushed himself up and paraded to the edge of the big pond. Kneeling, he leaned over to look into the water. At first he could only see the drowned forest at the bottom of it. Then he noticed a boy staring back at him. A live little boy at last!

"Hullo!" Peter said. But the boy said something at the same time and he couldn't hear him. "You go ahead," Peter said. But once again, the little boy looking back at him spoke when he spoke. A half a moment later, he knew how silly he had been. The little boy looking back could be none other than himself! But that couldn't be him. "You're much too big," he said as if he still spoke to a different boy. Then the other half of the moment struck him.

He ran back to Solomon Caw's tree, wondering so loudly in his head that he might have spoken aloud. 'How did this happen? What do I do?'

Either Solomon heard him or he anticipated the questions. "I told you to expect change when you change things, Peter."

"But I don't want to grow up!"

"It's too late for that. You've already begun."

"No!" cried Pan. "Why? Tell me why! Why now? What caused it?"

"When you asserted a new will, you shirked your responsibility. When you shirked your responsibility, you had a deeper understanding of how you had affected the world. When you saw how you affected the world and still refused to help it by continuing your bad form, you fell from grace. When you fell from grace, you blamed the world for hurting you and hence, the growing pains began."

Peter Pan sat in silence for a while. Solomon Caw waited patiently as the child mulled over what he had just heard. Eventually the boy spoke. "So," he began, reasoning it out aloud in his own way, "because I feel hurt by the way things changed in the world, I now must grow up?"

"That's only part of it," the crow said.

"Then why," continued Peter, "did I not start growing up when my mother barred the window and got another little boy to replace me? I felt hurt when things changed then, too."

Solomon cleared his throat. "Your mother, not you, is responsible for initiating that change. And that's the part you missed, you see. Responsibility. When you identified yourself with the inevitable hurt by the choices you made, you disturbed the contents of your mind. Part of growing up is learning you must be accountable for impinging upon the world. Once you start that process, you start to grow up."

Once more, Peter stewed over the words of Solomon Caw. Then he asked, "If I start doing my duty again, will I stop growing up?"

"I'm afraid not."

"Then how do I make it stop?"

"You cannot. Quite frankly, you are the only one I have ever known who ever stopped it at all. Also quite frankly, I have no idea how you managed it in the first place!"

"So how do I do stop it in the second place?"

"Perhaps you just don't want to listen. Now that it has begun, it must continue."

"But I don't want to grow up!" he cried more emphatically than ever.

"I know," Solomon coughed. He seemed pensive for a time. Then he added, "Perhaps it had been wrong of me to..." But Caw's words trailed off.

"Wrong of you to what?"

Solomon Caw sighed, then said, "I just wonder what might have been if I hadn't fulfilled your parents' request for another little boy. Perhaps you would have stayed with them and none of this –"

"You! You did this to me!" This thought had never occurred to Peter Pan before. Certainly Solomon Caw is responsible for the little boy that took his place!

"You cannot blame me! I did not have much choice, Peter Pan. You already had a wonderful life in the Gardens. Secondly, you could have stayed with your mother the first time the fairies allowed you to return. Am I wrong?" He watched as Peter lowered his head. "And lastly, your mother had her desire. I don't just give out children whenever I please. It must happen naturally. Should I have let your mother remain unhappy because of your bad form? She had a right to be happy, just as you were happy here."

"That's just it. I *had been*." Peter said nothing more about the matter. "So what am I to do now?"

"Time will tell. Now please, Peter Pan, let me sleep. I need my rest."

With a heavy heart and a literal growing problem, the small boy walked away to sit under the tree he once fit inside. He put his fists in his eyes and sobbed.

Chapter 3

Alternatives

Peter Pan had decided to ignore the new state of affairs. But try as he may, he could not do so on account of the fact that he just kept growing. He talked it out with the stars, but they only blinked in bewilderment. He also tried to go about things as usual. But the usual had become unusual some time ago. He could not go back to his chores for they would not solve his trouble. He still resented having no one to play with and the thought of forever quieted children depressed him. Besides, he could no longer figure out how to be a spirit so as to go part of the way with the children, and even if he could, perhaps a bigger child such as himself would frighten them anyway. He could not ride the goat, though he did sometimes find pleasure in playing, jumping, petting and running with it. Solomon Caw must have had a chat with the birds and animals, for they all seemed reassured of him being the same boy with whom they had previously frolicked. The fairies also appeared to have gotten used to his toddler size. Peter did not seem to care, or rather it is more true he remained oblivious, that the fairies used magic to keep him hidden from sight during the day. But he would soon find out.

One night when Peter awoke, he delightedly saw on the ground next to him an invitation-card to a fairy ball. He picked it up and began to read. It is more correct to say he tried to read as he found that he could not make out any of the letters. Even the 'P.P.' at the end of it indicating that he would be playing at the event looked unfamiliar to him. He wondered if just the hand-printing on this card caused his trouble. He knew a way in which he could check.

He made a long trek, down the Flower Walk, over the shadowy greens of pathways, to south of the Round Pound all the way over to the graves he had dug the year before. He stared and stared but to his dismay, the markings on these, too, (even though he had made them) were now just lines! 'Perhaps I have gotten too old already,' Peter thought. 'People forget things when they are old, or so I think I have heard.' Indeed, one of the little girls whom he chatted with ever so briefly one night had spoken at length about her grandfather. She loved him dearly, she had said, but if he didn't forget the simple things like the name of the book you're reading or on which day they have laundry he would have been more fun to have around.

Pan sighed, mourning his lost ability and the fact that it made him seem ever so old. So he went in search of some fairies to ask them the details of the party. He did not have to go far before he saw some flitting about. In fact, they were stretching out some mushrooms to use as tables for the very same party. He thrust the invitation card at them.

"Is this for tonight?"

"We're busy! Look for yourself!" snapped a lady fairy.

"I would, but, you see, I seem to have forgotten how to make sense of the marks."

"Pity," she replied.

"Yes, for tonight," said another. "You may as well stay here, for we are to begin soon."

"Did you bring your pipes?" asked a third.

"I can go fetch them." And he scooted off.

When he'd moved out of earshot the first fairy smacked the third. "You know very well he does not need his pipes!"

"But shall we not keep up the pretense? I venture we don't need this table-cloth, either," came the reply as the fairy watched the lady servants whisking their skirts so that the blossoms that had been shaken to the ground became a tablecloth. Then she threw a petal at the first fairy. An all-out fight broke out among the three of them.

Peter returned and scolded them. "I should like to think that you could keep your own grand manners, dear fairies!"

Either they realized his correctness or they heard the trumpets signaling the arrival of Queen Mab, or both. Whichever incident stopped the fighting, it did indeed cease, just as the Queen's entourage came upon the table. In a short while, a throng of fairies had gathered. Some began to grumble about there being nothing on the table as of yet. The others knew what would happen next.

Peter, of course, did not know what would happen next either so he began opening ceremony music on his pipes. As he seemed to get bigger even as they watched, a great many fairies looked at him with wide eyes. They disguised their gasps as coughs and ignored him thereafter. The boy did not notice the reactions, so engulfed in his notes.

"Peter Pan!" came the voice of Queen Mab.

Peter played on.

"Peter!" she shouted.

Still just music.

"PAN!"

The shout roused the boy's attention and he lowered his instrument. "Your highness?"

"Perhaps you failed to observe that there is no food laid out on the table."

"I suppose I noticed, but I forgot to mention it. I figured you knew what you were doing so I just played for you."

"Well, without any more ado I can tell you," Queen Mab said, "that your music will not be necessary this evening."

The fairies managing the table earlier gave each other severe glances and sneers.

"But why? Are you not to have a gala?" asked Pan.

"No festivities this night. We just wanted to get you in front of the fairy assemblage. We have something to discuss with you."

Peter sat down. "Are you cross with me?" he asked, thinking he detected some disenchantment in her tone.

"Not exactly with *you*. For as far as we can tell, you're doing it without trying."

Peter gulped, for he now had an idea as to what she referred. "I won't do it anymore," he said, knowing it to be a lie.

Queen Mab looked the boy up and down. "Perhaps you have guessed what I am talking about, Pan. And I must now tell you what we plan to do about it."

A new thought came to the lad. "You are to use magic and make me stop!" exclaimed Peter. He suddenly felt better. Why, he should have thought of this before!

"No. We cannot do that."

Peter felt like a smashed bird egg. "Why won't you?"

"If we speak of the same, then it is not a matter of won't so much as *can't*."

Peter's mood did not improve. He lay down on his back, looking up at the stars instead of the fairies surrounding him. "What is it, then, that *you* are talking about?"

"You are...well...getting bigger."

"Yes," said Peter sadly. "That's what I mean. But I am now thinking you could stop me growing up."

"Silly! Even *I* do not have the power to stop *that*!"

Peter sighed. "Then what is it that you called me for here and now?"

"That is just it. You shouldn't be here and now."

Pan darted upward like a spring released. "What?"

"I'm sorry, Peter Pan, but having you in the Gardens is just too big a risk. You are not aware, but we have had to use magic to conceal you from the rest of the world."

"But...I just come out after Lock-out Time! If I...I'll be more careful!"

"It is not just your growing that unsettles us. You, as of late, have been curt, gloomy and grumpy. We simply do not need that in and around the Gardens. 'Tis bad enough humans run around here with those feelings. Likewise, we do not need to be exerting so much magic to make sure you are unseen."

"But –"

"Hear this," she said. A silence like none of them had ever experienced fell over the crowd. Even the trees stopped rustling. Queen Mab broke the void. "Peter Pan, you may stay in Kensington Gardens no longer."

Prolonged gasps came from the gathering, some from birds and critters that had come to observe and some from leaves that shivered and some from, of course, fairies.

Peter stood in silence and a hush lingered, but not so great a quiet as the one that just passed. He dropped his pipes. He plopped down on his behind, buried his head in his hands and sobbed. He sobbed so much that the fairies near him had to be handed leaves to serve as umbrellas. Surely those with wings could have flown out of the way, but none of the little folk wanted to disturb the scene or lose their place. They all waited as Peter Pan shook and cried.

Queen Mab expected this kind of a response from him, so she let him go on but soon had her fill. "Peter..." she called.

Peter sobbed, "Leave me alone. You're kicking me out!"

"Peter Pan, we don't *want* to. We *must*. Please understand."

"I don't understand anything anymore," he said through heavy tears.

"Pan! Please listen, for I have more to say."

Peter wiped his eyes and rubbed his nose on his arm. "What more?"

"We offer you a solution."

Peter rubbed his nose again with one hand as the other thruked away another tear. A fairy had to dart out of the way of the splash. "You mean I can stay?"

"I told you no."

Peter groaned.

"Do you remember, Peter Pan, when we fairies granted the wish of your heart?"

"Of course I do. It's one of my well-known adventures!"

"Do you recall that we encouraged you to make a bigger wish? But you insisted –"

"On two little wishes. And you granted them both."

"They were the same wish, really," she muttered under her breath. "Well, Peter Pan, I'm afraid I hadn't been entirely honest with you that day."

"Oh?" Peter said, so taken aback that he leaned backward.

"You see, I could not bring myself to tell you."

"Tell me what?"

The Queen floated into the air. "Two little wishes do not equal one big wish."

"Oh," said Peter matter-of-factly. "Then what does equal one big wish?"

"Three, of course," she answered, flitting about him.

"Ah," said Peter.

"Do you know what that means?" she asked coming up behind at his ear.

"Why weren't you honest?"

"Because we wanted you to stay. We were afraid to lose you to your actual home. You were the one who claimed it to be two wishes. If we confessed and gave you the three, you might have been able to wish to go home once and for all."

"But I did! It's just that –"

"Yes, yes. We all know how it went," Queen Mab said as she hurried around him. "I ask again, do you know what it means?"

"What?"

Queen Mab waved her wee little fists in the air, her skirt wriggled and bounced as she alighted on a mushroom. "Think Peter. We gave you two wishes but…"

Peter saw it now. "Why, I have another wish left!"

"Exactly."

"I wish not to grow up!" he said triumphantly.

The fairies all sighed.

Queen Mab shook her head. "I told you, Pan, I do not have the power to do that."

"Besides," interrupted Colandrion, flying out. "Do you really think that is such a wise wish at this point?"

"Why not?"

"You wish to play with real boys. Well, Peter, does it not make sense to be a little older so as to befriend them better? Older boys know a lot better games," replied Colandrion.

Peter cocked his head. "I suppose that is true. But alas, there are never any boys!"

"I told you, Pan, I do not have the power to do that."

43

Queen Mab took to the air again. "Peter Pan, let us get back to your wish. I have a suggestion as to –"

"I wish for friends!" Peter blurted.

"I cannot grant that request either. Rather I *will* not."

Peter stuck out his tongue.

"Behave or I'll mischief you. Now, may I suggest your third wish?"

Most people are inclined to think dreams can come true. Even if they aren't so inclined, no one can honestly prefer the contrary. It's a fair notion, especially since fairies know it to be so. But they are as forthcoming about such matters as they are with visibility to grown-ups. Surely it's not surprising fairies can attest to fulfilled dreams. It's hardly a flight of fancy that they'd keep someplace sustained by fantasy. Indeed they do! And just like themselves, this place to call their own arises from children. Whether a rousing pretend during the day's playtime, or tucked in at night safe under the covers with night-lights burning bright, children are avid dreamers. In sum, multiple dreams add up and if any fraction of these spring to life in the division between slumber and awake, they reach a common denominator. But it's not worth musing on mathematics, since the sort who dream of arithmetic are not likely (apart from a precocious youth here or there) the sort who fixate on fairies. Nevertheless, a dream quota quotient remainder winds up on an island in the far ocean from London.

This island does not appear on any chart or map. So don't go looking for it – you'll easily sail right by without a glance. If you suppose looking directly will make the island appear, you're not as well versed in fairy magic as you might have thought. Tucked under cloud covers with stars as night-lights, this virtual dream land plays host to magical objects, entities and vegetation.

Settling back into her royal seat, Queen Mab said, "So you see, Peter Pan, brewed as you are in magic, we seem left with no choice but to send you to the Never, Never, Never Land."

"Come again?"

"The imagination island," said Colandrion.

"Ask me again!" he said as if he had just seen some great sleight-of-hand trick and wanted to watch one more time.

"Do you wish to live in the Never, Never, Never Land?"

"Never…"

The fairies let out sounds of either discontent or shock.

Peter said, "I did not answer, sillies. Never, Never, Never Land…do you really need all those Nevers? Isn't one Never as much as anyone needs?"

Chatting arose among the fairies, some in agreement with Pan and some in defense of the repetition, while still others agreed shortening it to just two had a nice ring to it. But Queen Mab settled them down with a wave of her hands.

"Is it one word?" asked Peter Pan.

"What?" asked Colandrion.

"If it is two words, it rather sounds like a command. Never Land. Is it a command?"

"Oh for goodness' sake!" Colandrion said, lowering his face into his hand.

Queen Mab decreed with a huff, "Very well! You may make it one word if you like, Peter Pan!" She composed herself. "Do you wish to live in the Never-Never Land?"

"Oh, yes, I will go!" The very idea of having someplace to go! He couldn't have hoped for more. Despite all the effort of wondering, he could never think of anywhere on his own.

The Queen flew up out of her throne (much to the relief of the street fairies holding it aloft who had rather enjoyed their break during all those loathsome explanations and wanted to get back to lollygagging) and sat upon the hand that Peter put out for her. "Don't be so quick to say yes."

Her majesty spoke with concern. Despite being a place of dreams the Never-Never Land is not always charming and dandy, no matter how hard one may hope. As much as there exists the adorable, fanciful and whimsical there's just as much of the abominable, frightening and worrisome. For not all dreams are pleasant, and nightmares also shape the isle.

As of late a different kind of unrest had found its shores. Two groups of people navigated to the island. Both came by sea, which is not really all that surprising as the only other way to reach the Neverland is by air.

The first visitors, seafarers by nature, were bound to come sooner or later. Though their glory days have waned, they are certainly still formidable foes to all they encounter including the valiant British fleet. Their reputation precedes them in any sea adventure worth its salt — pirates! Woe to those who cross their path.

The others chose a long and arduous ocean voyage over the turmoil in their land. They sought refuge from those that tormented them — yet another group of people who treated them in ways akin to piracy. Sad to say, but these would-be pirates are none other than settlers from Britain. Alas, the irony! The long and short of it: a particular tribe among the people with skin of red hue made their way across the ocean and reached those magical shores.

There's no way to say for sure how the pirates or the Redskins managed to find the fairy grounds. Perhaps the magical isle reflects the world's changes. The blame might be placed on the children, as pirates and Redskins crept into their playtime and fears. Or it could be they'd been called forth by the island itself. It matters very little, since they are now permanent additions to the chaos.

Colandrion provided more details on both pirates and Redskins, and Peter Pan listened eagerly. He rather liked the idea of captains and chiefs, crews and tribal customs. But the thought of being among such people did seem rather perilous, even though it sounded like a grand adventure.

"And you want *me* to go *there*? I'm just a little boy!"

At this point, Queen Mab flew into his face. "No, Peter Pan! You are a *wonderful* boy!"

"I am?" he squealed with delight.

"You defied the very laws of Nature. You look after Kensington Gardens. You have nearly been to the hereafter. You speak with birds. You tamed a goat. You have flown. You can play the grass moving and call forth the moonlight on your pipes. You are a fairy friend! Peter, why else have you been bestowed the name of a Nature deity?"

"I *am* a wonderful boy!" Pan exclaimed with more delight. But the next moment he asked, concerned, "If I go to the Neverland, will I stop aging?"

"How many times must we tell you?" Colandrion replied.

"A thought…" said Queen Mab aloud and then paused far too long as all eyes turned to her, eager to hear what she'd say next, which turned out to be, "…the Never-Never Land, as such, may affect beings not created by dreaming."

"What of the pirates and Redskins?" asked Colandrion.

"We have never discerned much since the investigators always lose interest."

"I might stay young there?" he asked, stuck on the idea.

"Possibly, Peter," sighed Queen Mab, exhausted by the question.

Colandrion said, "I've heard that Solomon Caw believes a change in Peter's perception caused the growth. Could not a shift stop him again?"

A bright blue fairy from the intently listening crowd ventured, "Then it's just a matter of willing it?"

"It cannot be. For I have tried," Peter answered sadly.

"Well," replied Colandrion, "Doubt exists within you. Something must spark up from within you to shove out unsteady faith. A spark within, undoubtedly ignited from the outside."

"Like Jake disappearing! How cross I'd been! I made my decision and the next thing I knew —"

"Exactly," grinned Colandrion.

"So that settles it, somewhat," Mab decreed. "We'll have to see what actually does happen to him once he resides in the Never, Never, Never Land."

Even though Peter Pan knew it would infuriate the Queen, he said, "I cannot take the chance. I would rather my wish be for real boys as friends."

It did infuriate her fairy highness. "Be reasonable, Peter Pan. I do not wish to grant that wish. Please just say you will go to the Never-Never Land."

"I'm having doubts now myself," Colandrion said. "*Is* it wise to send a little boy to a place teeming with terrors?"

A hush fell upon them all.

"It's not just terrors. It's whimsy, too!" Mab argued.

"With all due respect, your Majesty," Colandrion said with a bow, "is it not you who warned Peter of danger?"

She answered, "But we've no other choice. We cannot satisfy all parts of this dilemma."

Another hush.

Colandrion broke the silence with a gleam in his eye. "We need another opinion."

Queen Mab knew what her courtier meant to say. "No. Out of the question."

"It is not, milady," he said with a wink. "We shall have to go below."

Chapter 4

Understanding

What could Colandrion have meant? Only Queen Mab and Colandrion himself seemed to know. The Queen stared at him quite long, just the right amount to make everyone uncomfortable. Then she said, "We need not call upon them. We shall not intermingle again!"

"Your highness, we are stymied because we are so close to the problem. We must seek wisdom outside of our own."

"Very well," she agreed. "But only I, you and Peter Pan shall go below."

Moans rang out from the crowd at the exclusion, for all wondered as much as Peter.

Queen Mab called off the mock-party. She had to forcefully flit about and threaten extra work detail to rouse some loitering fairies. Peter stopped a few of them and entrusted his pipes, requesting that they put the instrument in his tree. Once all were gone, Mab flew and gestured for Peter and Colandrion. Peter stood up, feeling taller, just as the Queen landed and began walking. As he followed along, Peter thought perhaps he might ask Mab the reason she didn't simply soar along in the air but he didn't want to spoil the adventure.

Near the bank of the Serpentine, a rustling of leaves came from the east, louder than leaves had any right to make, let alone that not many leaves reside so close to the ground in the particular area as a general rule. A large leaf rose up and revealed a small hand, which belonged to a little fellow, carrying a woven bark basket. "How do, your Highness!"

"Likewise, I'm sure. Didn't feel like attending the festivities again, Chetwin?"

"Much as I'd like to," answered Chetwin, "I thought it a private affair. Besides, someone has to pick up the invitation-cards strewn about." His round nose dotted his head perfectly. "Oh! Greetings, Peter Pan," he said as soon as he noticed.

"Hullo," said Peter without much effort. "I've not seen you before."

The wee roundish fellow said, "Though surely you know of street fairies?"

"I know of street fairies. Your kind can be rather a nuisance," Peter said, telling the truth with no remorse.

Chetwin laughed at the comment. "Indeed. Well, you may also call me a telluric fairy — fancy way of saying no wings, that. Some will say we're the riff raff, but don't let them fool you. We can bring about just as much mischief and fun as our airy cousins."

"You may tell him your mischief, Chetwin, for it is why we have come."

"You don't say!" exclaimed the round little man. He then said with great pride, "My sort's rather special among fairies, street or otherwise. We tend to the paths." He swung his arm in an enticing come hither gesture. "Follow me, Peter Pan. I've something to show you."

Peter could not resist and took solemn steps after him.

"Have you noticed smaller paths in the Gardens, Peter?"

"The ones wide at one part that become so narrow further down I am able to stand astride them with my legs?"

"Those are the very paths I mean. The Paths that have Made Themselves."

Peter's eyes brightened at such a magical thought.

"Most folks think they're just trying to get to the Round Pond. And yes, clearly they are. But some of them, just some of them, lead somewhere else."

Peter's interest piqued even more as he realized that Chetwin led him along a Path that had Made Itself, one that appeared on this side of the long lake and no doubt one of the select few that lead to somewhere new. But it only led him back to the Serpentine.

"Before you complain," said Chetwin, "all the difference has been made by following the path. Now, look into the water, Peter Pan. What do you see?"

"Rippling."

"And what besides the rippling?"

"Besides?"

"Look carefully, Peter."

"Oh. You mean the stars. And the trees all growing upside down."

Precisely like the moment we open a book and are unexpectedly greeted by an elaborate unfolding pop-up, all at once he could experience the forest sunken in the Serpentine. The image rippled all around him, appearing as a real place. A place he could smell, with grass he could feel under his toes. He blinked for a long moment. Out of the corners of his eyes, he saw the lights of Colandrion and Queen Mab.

A jovial, doddery voice called out, "Hullo! Hullo! Mercy! Loo Loo! Don't see fairy folk too often! Hullo again!"

Peter turned his head to see who had spoken and looked upon a small man, of sorts, standing at a podium with an enormous book and quill. The man looked over-characteristically old, so much so that he seemed young. He had a bald head, except for tufts of well-groomed straw-like hair over his pointed ears, complimented nicely by the straw hair jutting from his chin. He had a slightly long nose on which rested oval spectacles at the tip, one lens tinted rose. A teal and white sheen swam in his eyes. He wore a tailored yellow jacket in a faint paisley stained leaf print and matching waistcoat. Below his waist, he seemed not rather unlike an overgrown chipmunk with his little tail wagging.

"And who is this fine young lad? Loo loo. Looks mighty big already to be just down to the entrance. What's the buzz, fairy folk? What say you, stranger boy? Loo loo!"

"I am Peter Pan, the wonderful boy."

"Peter Pan, eh? Loo. I think I have you in my records." He laughed, "Well then, I would. I mean I must, mustn't I?" He flipped backward in the book, reading. Then he said, "Ah, yes! I should have known. Been awful busy with that project. Yes, loo, should have known." He laughed some more and then calmed a bit. "Loo loo. Pleased to finally meet you, Peter Pan! I am Clark Chauncer the Chronicler."

Peter Pan asked, "What is a 'chronicler'?"

"Loo loo. Don't you know where you are?" He waddled over and put out a hand.

Peter did not know, of course, about shaking hands, so he just touched what could have passed for a paw. "I am not even sure how I got here. A street fairy had me look at the water in the Serpentine and then…"

"Ah, yes. Of course. About time you spoke, Queen Mab. Surely you are purposed in coming down here! Loo."

"I am hesitant to be here at all, Clark Chauncer. But Colandrion here deems it best. Pray tell, might we have audience with Sylvanus?"

"Loo! Audience with! Let me check the books," he quickly waddled back to his podium with the large book. He flipped a few pages as he picked up his quill. He perused intently, then spoke. "Loo loo! Can squeeze you in, to be sure. Not right away, of course. But soon. Loo! Enough of a wait that you can have an explore with young Pan." He scribbled in the book and then began rapidly flipping and hunting through pages, grabbed a golden watch out of his pocket, said, "Loo loo!" and began scribbling again feverishly.

Peter stood as if lost in a London fog.

"Loo!" said Chauncer again while looking at another part of the book, reading. "Loo loo! Very well, Peter, now that I've reviewed the record, I –"

"What are you writing? What do you record?"

"Why, everything! Loo! Well, that is at least everything that matters enough as pertains both above and below in Kensington Gardens!"

"Is this place below the Gardens?"

"Loo loo! That it is, Peter Pan! The Drowned Forest of the Serpentine."

"You mean I'm under water?"

"In that vicinity. Loo loo."

"Is this a magical place?" asked Peter, looking at the stretch of foreboding forest ahead of him. Clark Chauncer, the podium and the large book resided just on the edge of the woods.

"Yes, Peter Pan," came the voice of Queen Mab. "Another *secret* magic location. We should leave Clark Chauncer to his work. He has graciously allowed us passage into the Drowned Forest. So we must go."

"Into the woods?"

"The same," cried Colandrion zipping toward the trees.

"Ta-ta!" Clark called.

Filled with wonder and a little caution, Peter followed Colandrion and Queen Mab into the forest. On his way in, a streak of grey whizzed past him. It had that same frosted glass quality as the one that took Jake away.

"There it is again!" Peter said.

Colandrion called back, "Let the Drowned Forest Dwellers do their work unless they stop to speak to you."

Unsatisfied, but feeling that such things would be explained soon enough, Peter Pan caught up to the fairies. They weaved in and around the mysterious depths of trees. Peter noticed that he really enjoyed the little twinge of terror that he felt inside. It is not really fair to call it terror. So instead it shall be described as a nervous delight. Peter Pan, on the cusp of an adventure, never wanted the thrill of exploring the ominous unknown to subside. Onward he walked, chasing after the white and mauve fairy lights. He caught the faint sound of clinking metal, adding sharp delight. "What's that?" he asked eagerly.

Queen Mab answered. "By the sound, he's busy, so we shall not bother him. We're looking for someone else…"

"Look!" exclaimed Peter. He pointed to an eddy of swirling leaves.

"Ah," said Queen Mab, "there he is now!"

As she said this, something stood in the whirlwind leaves. A basic human shape but with only one leg and the head of a dog, with a wagging tail completing the image. He had seen glimpses of dogs from the Gardens and also knew the bronze terrier who stands guard near the Palace Gate entrance to the Broad Walk. Peter clapped his hands. "How ripping!"

The dog-man spoke. "You who are not afraid, you will now –" but he cut short when he saw the fairies. "Why, Queen Mab! My, has it been a long time!"

"Good greetings, Arone. My I present Colandrion and a fairy friend –"

"By thunder! If it isn't Peter Pan!"

Peter relished the way the inhabitants knew him. He felt even more like a wonderful boy. "You know me?"

"Ay! I've longed to have you as a pupil!"

"He's not here for that," explained Queen Mab. "We await audience with Sylvanus."

"Pity. I should like to see what we can teach each other."

"Who are you?" asked Peter.

The dog-man bowed. "I am Mentor Arone. I teach the –"

The Queen tried to quiet him. "Don't say it!"

"– boys."

"Now you've done it," she drooped.

Peter burst with energy. "Boys! There are boys here?!"

"Lest we'd be left wondering what to do with ourselves!" Arone said in a laughing bark.

Peter looked at Queen Mab. "I want to stay here."

Arone barked again. "But no boys can *stay*!"

59

Peter harrumphed and trotted over to Arone. "You just said you teach boys."

"True. But they do not remain forever."

"But surely I can stay and play with them?"

Arone looked at him. "Mostly they are in lessons. Do you wish to take lessons?"

Lessons sounded entirely too solemn to Peter Pan. He thought back to when his parents mentioned lessons in the week before he flew away. "No, I do not wish for lessons. I want to play games."

"Lessons can be rather like games," replied Arone, winking at the boy. Far off metal still clinked.

"Couldn't I just see the boys?" asked Peter.

"Forgive him, Arone," Colandrion said. "He does not know the workings of the Drowned Forest and he has an obsession with being like and playing with a real boy."

"Ah," said Arone. "Well, Peter Pan, I should like very much to show you a real boy, but I cannot. I am sorry to have to tell you that these are not entirely real boys."

"What kind of boys are they?" questioned Peter, looking up into Arone's furry face.

Arone knelt down on his one knee. He placed a hand on Peter's shoulder. "So many questions you must have, Peter Pan, so many questions indeed," Arone said, tousling Peter's hair, for

Pan now had a great deal of it. Arone stood again, and hopped over to rest on a large boulder.

"Can anyone bring me a real boy?"

"Totally obsessed." Colandrion floated snidely away.

"I doubt we'd be able to grant your request."

"Why won't anyone let me?!" Peter whined.

"Poor Peter Pan," Queen Mab said sincerely.

Arone had a look of surprise, then he leaned over the side of the rock. "Look here!" He held up a piece of bark that had a sprig growing from it. "Surely a sign!"

"What is? A sign of what?" asked Peter.

Arone studied it carefully, ignoring the questions. Queen Mab whispered to Pan. "Don't worry about what he speaks of, Peter. It will only make sense to him and those who have attended his lessons." Peter longed to be privy as well.

Arone nodded to the bark and sprig and placed it back down. As soon as it touched the soil, the noise in the background ceased. "Their lesson has ended. Come, follow me," Arone said as he stood, "we may be able to catch them." He hopped vigorously away.

The two fairies and Peter Pan followed Arone's thrashing tail further into the forest. Though he did not have time to stop and examine it, Peter saw a clearing to his left with a great oval arena. Many flags flapped on poles lining the edge. A bit later on to his right he saw a humble home covered in leaves and moss. Deeper into the woods, but not before too long, Peter heard the giggling voices of little boys. He sped on ahead, pushing a peephole amid some leaves. He saw a number of boys. He would have been dumbstruck even at this sight alone. But an eerie coincidence kept him unable to move, despite all his valiant attempts. One of them looked just like Jake Mortimer Higgins!

Peter watched, frozen with joy. He finally summoned his voice and strength to move when suddenly his vision blurred, jolting him backward. The blurriness stopped and he could see that a bubble had passed before his eyes. It wafted a bit closer to him and popped. But instead of a faint ploop noise, it said softly, "Sylvanus awaits."

When he looked back toward the boys each and every one had inexplicably gone, along with their noise. Peter thought it rather cruel.

"Come, Peter," Queen Mab said.

He turned to her grumbling, "Oh, very well."

"You'd best not keep Sylvanus waiting," Arone told them. "Do you recall the way to his keep, Queen Mab?"

"I believe I do," she said.

Arone bowed to Peter as the boy walked toward Mab's flying light. "Take care, Peter Pan. Until we next meet!"

Peter waved goodbye and then ran to catch up to Mab as Colandrion flew up behind. "I just saw Jake!" Peter called back to Colandrion.

"We shall check with Clark Chauncer's records later. Just follow the Queen."

They headed westward, passing tree after tree, reminding Pan of the enveloping vastness of the Gardens. Shortly after too long, the trees closed in so as to become impassable. Peter watched with amazement as the fairy lights pushed straight into a large dark knothole. If they hadn't shown him the way, Peter would have been fooled. It had certainly looked solid! He remarked to himself about the cleverness of the powerful illusion. He decided then and there to forever be wary of such secrets in his surroundings.

When he moved to the "knothole," he discovered that despite his new size, he could crawl in with ease. After seven feet he came out the other side. Towering above him, partly shimmering like a spider web, he saw a great doorway woven from trees and covered in moss. The trees intermingled their branches, expanding from the door in a deliberate natural architecture. The decorative woven twigs went as far as the eye could see and dwarfed the trio of guests. They felt the very same way in which grains of sand do sitting so close to the ocean.

Before Peter Pan could have a proper reaction of any sort, there came a great noise of rushing water, but no water gushed and nothing got wet. Instead, he watched with awe as the massive moss-covered doors broke forth. Only just a crack but they needed no more for this crack spanned nearly two times Peter's length, and thus, more than ample for him and the fairies to enter the gates.

A dewy mist rose up and when it cleared, Peter rubbed his eyes for it stung a bit. A thick stream of sunlight angled down, illuminating a tree stump. Looking up toward its source only revealed what looked like the surface of the water from underwater. A golden hue cast over the stump and the cluster of plants and weeds that encircled it. The stump itself proved truly amazing and Peter marveled at how it seamlessly blended into a stone column from days of yore, betwixt-and-between those two things. Ivy curled around it and a solid gold ring encircled the top before the pillar plateaued.

Sunlight flared up and Peter could see a shape forming as if an outline thickened and before too long, Sylvanus himself sat on the plateau of the column. Peter marveled once more. Sylvanus's long, spindly, furry and cloven legs bent at the knees, reaching practically to his chest. Equally long arms curled around his legs. Very long pointed ears protruded out of wild bark-like hair with lots of many different leaves on his elongated head. A very large acorn topper sat on his head, situated just so between large and browning antlers. His black and large eyes, swooshing around like murky puddles, possessed of a friendly wealth of understanding and knowledge. A long moss beard unfurled and he spoke as he unfolded.

"Salvere Jubere! Welcome, Peter Pan! Clark Chauncer has regaled me with tales of you. At last I gaze upon you myself."

Peter Pan bowed.

By this time Sylvanus stood, spanning a full sixteen feet tall. Peter Pan suddenly knew how the fairies must feel in the presence of full-grown humans. Pan walked over to the stump-column, climbed it with ease, sat down and examined his surroundings bathed in the golden churning rays.

Sylvanus laughed like a cricket chirping. "Make yourselves at home, surely!"

The fairies flew up higher to be on eye level with Sylvanus. Mab spoke with reminiscence in her voice. "It has been some time."

The woodland entity kept his joviality as he said, "So long, I fear, that I venture no one left on the surface world has heard of me. Present company excepted, of course." He crossed his gangly arms. "So, Queen Mab, you do not come into my keep, as I recall, unless you want something from me." He leaned closer to her, "What did you need last time? Oh yes. *Now* what's the matter? Longevity got you down?"

"Pshaw! I'm good forever," laughed the Queen.

"Then I suppose," Sylvanus said, turning to Peter, and bending his legs to sit on his haunches, "that the boy Pan is not merely visiting."

"We have come for advice," Queen Mab explained. "We have reached a stalemate regarding Pan's future."

"If Clark Chauncer's reports are to be believed, and there is no reason they should not, the lad is growing up," Sylvanus said and even though he braced himself, Peter winced at the words. "I know as much as that. To say nothing of the burden he's caused to those who dwell in Kensington Gardens."

"Just as you say," said Colandrion, flapping down to the stump-column next to Peter. "We're thinking we must send the boy Pan to the Never-Never Land."

At this remark Sylvanus's expression turned to that of hearing about someone enrolled at an esteemed school.

Colandrion continued, "Yet we know what folly there may be in doing so."

"But that's not the whole problem," added the Queen. "For Peter Pan, you see, wishes for something else altogether. Go on, Peter. Tell him what you want."

"Real boys. To have adventures with them. I know you have some! Can't I stay with a few of them?"

Sylvanus laughed and sighed at the same time, sounding like crickets at different speeds. "Now I see." He paused, then looked to the little shining white light. "Tell me, Mab, does Pan know the purpose of the Drowned Forest?"

"Not unless he's pieced it together."

"So tell me," insisted Peter, pointing a finger at Mab.

"That honor," she said, "belongs to Old Sylvanus himself."

With a few creaks and rustles, Sylvanus stretched himself upright. His throat cleared like a flock of birds taking off. "This may seem strange," he said in solemn tone and then waited until sure he commanded attention.

"*This may seem strange.*"

67

He inundated the little tot with a cyclical yet sidetracked harangue which can be summed up more or less in this way: Sometimes children (mostly if not always boys) fall out of their perambulators when the nurse is looking the other way and if they are not claimed in seven days they are sent away to defray expenses. It's undoubtedly authorized as the truth. But as with any truth, there's often more of it to be found lurking about. The rest, as told by Sylvanus, branched out into many specifics and Pan lost interest. He began to listen again when he heard mention of a mysterious place with no yesterday, no tomorrow and no today. Peter recalled being in such a place not too long ago, adrift in his boat.

We have all heard the adage about stopping to smell roses, but few realize its true potential in the pursuit of the eternal soul, chi, purusha, ka, dosha, animus... but just as Shakespeare so simply said about the rose, the riddle of existence is none less sweet. Children, however, often smell in excess, and the scent of never-ending swirls of adventure linger about them like a haze.

Peter Pan (sounding sufficiently bored and slouching) said, "So the Drowned Forest is the place for boys who have gotten too wound up."

Sylvanus chuckled like cicadas chirping. "That's a fair description. When a boy falls by the wayside, Clark Chauncer takes note and gives word to Nickert."

"Nickert?"

"I hear his grey blur has swished by you. He's a swift fellow who snatches up a boy's adventurous side and brings it to the Drowned Forest," he said.

Now the wrong impression mustn't be made of Nickert and his duties. Though it may sound perfectly dreadful to have part of them snatched away, rest assured that the boys are perfectly well, albeit very self absorbed. If you have ever seen a boy sitting under a tree with a vacant expression, you can believe he's been paid a visit from quick Nickert in the past.

At this turn of events, Sylvanus observed a sudden keen interest from Peter. "What happens next?" Pan asked, developing a fondness for story time now that it proved more exciting.

"The boy wanders the sunken forest until out of the wilderness comes Arone, a one-legged, dog-headed..."

"I met him!" exclaimed Peter, feeling important to have done so, as if he were part of the wild tale being told.

You might expect running in terror to be the natural reaction to such a sight. And most times it's a safe bet. The boy is scared into his wits rather than out of them and thus retreats to the daily routine. But for some boys (Peter Pan especially) a dog-headed, one-legged fellow is a boon — a real-life adventure in the making. Unable to resist, boys follow. What a dire situation! Or it would be, if strolling into danger did not provide such fun. While the boy is unable to see the forest for the trees, the Drowned Forest dwellers make use of the time before he leaves, which can be no more than the aforementioned seven days. If you're wondering about that, you're in luck, for it happens to be what misfocused Peter Pan asked about next.

"Why is it only seven days?"

Sylvanus said nearly apologetically, "I do not know. It is just authorized that way. You spent the same amount of time at home before you began your great escape to Kensington Gardens, did you not? It's often considered a lucky number. Is either reason significant? We can only venture a guess."

If rescued from wit's end before the seven days are up, a boy might, later on in life, discover that he knows something useful such as the right time to pick honeysuckle on a summer's evening or how to land that perfect punch to defeat a bully in a park. Pleased with himself, he will take credit for the knowledge without so much as a nod to where he learned it. For the Drowned Forest itself seems no more than one of the many fantasies of a child's mind.

If the seven days pass, however, a boy will still reconnect, but not without a price. A part of him will always remain waterlogged and some of the sharper edges of his mental maps will have smoothed out. From then on, he's not very focused. After all, an imaginexplosion is bound to make anyone a little muddled. He leaves a mark in fantasy, which he can never reclaim.

And all the while, Clark Chauncer chronicles what happens, above and below.

Pan asked, "What happens to the mark he leaves behind?"

"Well, Peter, we have no choice but to send it back to the neither-here-nor-when place. But that mucks up the works, like a clock ebbing slowly away from true time." He paused, then said, "Which brings me to my solution."

Queen Mab flew up, excitement shattering her yawning. "Just what I wanted to hear."

Sylvanus resumed pacing on his lanky legs. "Peter Pan, the fairies once again graciously offer you a place to live. Obey. Go to the Never-Never Land."

Peter stuck out his tongue and turned up his nose, for he did not like the Queen's choice winning out, especially since it meant losing his chance to stay in the Drowned Forest and make friends.

"But what of the risks?" asked Mab, now concerned.

"You must give him an advantage."

Wariness controlled her and she asked slowly, "What advantage?"

"Flight."

Mab protested, sounding fearful, "But he will only –"

"Permanently," Sylvanus added.

Mab clenched her fists.

Colandrion listened with great interest.

"He'll need to fly," advised the wise old sage, "if only to collect the marks left behind to defray expenses to the world above. And what better place for that than your magical isle?" His audience looked on with great wonderment, so Sylvanus went on, "The island manifests children's imagination and dreams, does it not? Perhaps the reverse holds true. I'm hoping if Peter Pan brings what has fallen from the prams, the Never-Never Land will prove powerful enough to harbor the real and whole boy on its wondrous shores."

The trio of visitors pondered his notion. After a bit, the forest fellow spoke again. "Long have I wanted to try. But sending little boys to the harsh realities of the island alone seemed too cruel. With friend-of-the-fairies Peter Pan to look out for them, though, well, that's a bark of another tree. After all, does he not have experience comforting scared children?"

"So," Peter asked, just to make sure he didn't make-believe it, "I shall be able to fly and forever play with friends in the Neverland?"

"That's right," creaked Sylvanus.

Peter Pan danced about, not even needing music.

Try as she might, Queen Mab could not find a flaw in Sylvanus's plan. She did not so much enjoy the idea of providing the little boy with constant flight. But besides the edge he'd have over the isle's newcomers, it would also allow visits to the Gardens. The more she thought, the less she could refuse. "A reasonable compromise. I accept. But I have a question."

"Why don't girls fall out of their prams?" Peter interjected, stopping his dance immediately.

"Well, Pan, it's simple," answered Sylvanus. "Girls are more grounded. So it is difficult for them to get lost in the clouds. Not impossible, I suppose. But it hardly if not never seems to happen at such a tender age. Rather clever, girls are."

"Oh. Will I grow up in the Neverland, Sylvanus?"

Queen Mab literally jumped in, landing on Peter's head. His soft, thick tufts of hair tickled her feet. "My question is nearly the same. It won't behoove either Pan or the island to be burdened with a gaggle of infants."

Sylvanus replied, "Believe it or not, Clark has recorded growth among the boys in our charge. Their age seems determined by their progress within the seven days. Those who come to their senses, well, Clark reports them to be the sort who act very mature for their age and cannot wait to be grown ups." (Peter Pan shuddered at the very idea.) "Not surprisingly you'll find they match up with sparrows pretending to be thrushes, as I understand Solomon Caw still pulls that trick from time to time. At any rate, until Pan fetches them, they'll size according to how they behave. As for you, Peter Pan, I cannot be sure if you will grow up in the Never-Never Land." Another silence held for a moment too long. "Is the matter closed then? We are in agreement with the predicament's solution?" They all nodded. "Then I bid you farewell."

"One last bit," said Peter. "Jake. I saw him down here."

"Ah, yes, the Higgins boy."

"Nickert took Jake right out from under my nose. His body had gone, too. Why? Is he a *whole* boy here?"

"A special case, Higgins. Nickert took advantage of a rare opportunity. He stole him in an attempt to further understand the correlation betwixt —"

"I do not understand," Pan interrupted. "But no matter. May I play with Jake?"

Sylvanus only said, "Jake is safe." He turned to the wee folk. "Queen Mab and fairy courtier, take care of yourselves and this boy," he said with a kind of salute. "Peter Pan," he said as he crouched down, his elongated frame bunching up, "it has been the utmost pleasure to make your acquaintance. Hail to thee, wonderful boy of the Never-Never Land!"

Peter bowed.

"Now, kindly get off my stumpillar," Sylvanus laughed with a bee buzz.

Peter obliged and watched the gangly furry hooved legs nimbly jump up onto the stumpillar. Sylvanus folded himself again, his antlers looking as if they reached the sky. With a slight breeze, he vanished from sight.

"Well," said Peter. "Let's go see if we can find Jake."

Queen Mab shot into his face. "No! We're going back to the Gardens."

Chapter 5

Lessons

The visitors checked in with Clark Chauncer on their way out and decided the teachers of the Drowned Forest would have to make time to train Peter. If Pan would live in the Neverland, then surely he would need training in the art of battle and the ways of Nature. This prospect sounded entirely too delicious to Peter. And being able to fly — whenever he pleased! But what brought him even more joy is remembering to ask Clark about Jake. While Queen Mab rolled her eyes, Clark Chauncer pacified Peter with information about Higgins like his being one of the best pupils in an unearthly long time. In fact, the last time any boy matched his skill went so far back in

Clark's great tome that he did not even bother thumbing through it. More to the point, Clark guaranteed some allotted time for Pan to see, speak and play with Jake. According to the Chronicler, there were no plans to send the boy Higgins anywhere. Nickert had not completed his study of the lad and no further action regarding his future could be taken without his consent. Clark checked the scheduling and they decided Peter should return to the Drowned Forest after three days. Peter Pan felt beside himself with joy.

Once back in Kensington Gardens, Peter ran for his tree. He reached in and grabbed his pipes. He danced and played, more gaily then he had in what seemed longer than forever. He pranced and skipped about, joined by some fairies and some chipmunks. The chipmunks made him think of his new friend Clark, along with a flow of memories resulting in dancing and piping harder. Soon his goat danced alongside him. Before long he tuckered himself out, but he still felt far from tired.

He wanted to tell of his adventures. Dancing fairies would only pretend to be interested in what had just happened to him, but he had to tell someone. He knew just where to go. He ran as fast as he could, stopping to pant at the base of a certain tree.

"Solomon! Solomon! I have great news!" he called.

But no reply came.

"Solomon! Wake up! I have wonderful news!"

Still no answer. Peter raised his pipes to his lips to blow a note so as to rouse the crow. Just about to make the sound, he received a response. But Solomon Caw had not been the one who responded. A young crow hopped down onto the branch.

"Hullo, Peter Pan."

"Good evening. May I speak with Solomon Caw?"

The crow cawed once, then said, "Would that you could."

"Is he cross with me? I shall make amends."

"Too late, I'm afraid." The little crow hopped further along the branch toward Peter. With sadness in his voice, he continued, "Solomon Caw now nests in the other place."

"Solomon is in the Drowned Forest?"

"The Drowned Forest! Dear no. The *other* place, Peter."

Peter gasped. The stocking had been taken down, too.

"He would not want you to weep for him. He certainly lived a longer and fuller life than any other bird. He finally came to retire as he so wanted." But it seemed little comfort to Peter, thrucking away a tear as he had not made peace with him.

The crow sensed his unease and said, "Ah, perhaps I can ease your pain. I have been working with Solomon since I came from the egg. He always spoke glowingly of you. Said you added a much needed chaos to the mundane." He cocked his head.

Pan asked, "Will there be no one to take his place?"

"Silly boy! I shall. I told you, I have been understudying him. Fear not, Solomon taught me well. Now, if you will excuse me, due to the tenderness of the situation surrounding his last hours, Solomon and I left much unattended. Much work to catch up on."

"All right," said Peter, "but I don't know your name."

"Thaddeus."

"Best of luck to you, Thaddeus Crow. You already have Caw's comforting manner. I just feel you shall be good at responsibility."

"Thank you, lad! May fortune smile on you as well." With that, Thaddeus flew back up into the tree and cawed a goodbye caw.

"Thaddeus."

As Peter walked away from the tree, his thoughts turned to Solomon. Unlike a fairy, he mixed up emotions all at once. Sad, of course, but a sweet sadness, for Peter felt glad that Solomon did finally receive his retirement, even if from the world entirely. Solomon Caw must have had something enchanted about him, for how else would he have been fulfilling requests for so long? Peter wondered at this enchantment. Perhaps he himself had a bit of it, too. It proved comforting and he curled up to sleep.

The next night a fairy ball whooped up. Peter attended and happily provided the entertainment. By this time, word had spread among the fairies about the situation of Peter Pan and the festivities soon became a farewell party for him. But they were not fooling anyone, for they all knew that there might always be just one more good-bye party.

And in fact, despite the lateness of hour to which this party lasted, another goodbye gala sprang up the very next night! What's more, this party started much earlier, on account of those tricky telluric fairies climbing up and changing the hour on the board for Lock-out Time. Shortly after, Peter Pan strolled down to the Serpentine. He peered in, smiling at the upside-down trees. He shook with excitement, wanting to be a part of the water so he planned on a drift in his boat.

To his great dismay, he discovered himself entirely too big for it. A tot who could not even kneel in the large Thrush Nest. He sighed. He sat down on the bank and put his feet in the water. He swoshed around in it, thinking of what his life would be soon. He drifted to how his warring lessons might be. Meandering his thoughts even more, he imagined standing up to the perils in the Neverland. He filled with confidence. He leaned over and looked again into the water. He dove. Now that his arms and legs were bigger, he did not find it so difficult to maneuver in the water. In fact, he kept his head above with ease, in a kind of dog paddle. With a little practice, swimming would be no challenge for him. Quite pleased with himself, Peter floated lazily about.

A gathering of critters and fairies applauded his action, even the two cormorants there on holiday and a moorhen who had recently gained control of the area by incessant warbling. Then some ducks swam his way. They had a look in their eye that showed Peter their disdain for the invasion of their domain. If the truth is to be known, they never got used to the large nest sailing around but now it seemed by their quick quacks they would prefer it.

Not wanting to waste the chance to show off his new ability to his friends, Peter pushed himself to do more. He summoned some courage and dunked his head. He stayed under.

He popped back out again. This simple little feat meant a great deal to him. But he had enough for the moment. He could see the ribbons in the distance and a gathering throng of fairies ready with their preparations for the party to be held in his honor. So he pushed his way through the water, back to the shore. Dripping wet, he felt a chill. He shook himself like a dog in an attempt to dry himself. It didn't really work, but he didn't care and went off to the party. A revelry in every sense wore on into the night.

And then, to the surprise of no one, another party arose on the third night. The buzz circulated that this had to be the actual farewell celebration as Peter would begin his training the next morning. It meant they would have to be sure to end the festivities at a reasonable hour. Peter Pan needed to get some rest that night. For in the wee hours of the morning with grey still out, before Kensington Gardens opened again, Peter Pan would return to the Drowned Forest.

This third party proved even merrier than the last two, as a few new concoctions spread across the table. And best of all, they sampled all three kinds (blackthorn, berberris and cowslip) of Queen Mab's wines! Quite curious, Peter took a sip from the berberris bottle. Definitely too sharp for him. He did not like it one bit. And since drinking at a party felt like a grown-up thing to do anyway, he decided to leave the drinking to the small folk.

Then, perhaps the drinking made him do it, but Colandrion stood on a mushroom. Though his speech touched on what one might expect from being filled with wine, such as loving them all and being so proud of Peter and the course things have taken, he spoke true. How he would miss having their little Betwixt-and-Between around! The crowd responded with agreeing cheers. Colandrion said, "Peter Pan, you must come visit us from time to time."

"Oh I shall. I will need to collect the boys, don't you remember?"

"Ah, yes, well. I am glad for that."

"As am I," said Peter, reaching for his pipes.

"And don't worry about the outside world knowing of you," said a tipsy Queen Mab, "for you can be sure, Peter, that we fairies will bring your tale to the ears of the children who come to the Gardens. And then they will tell their friends and so it will go on so long as there are children."

"I so love the idea that those outside the Gardens have heard of me!"

"I know. Now, play that song. You know which one."

And he did.

When the party came to an end, Peter went to his tree. He curled up under it, leg arched. For some time he seemed almost too excited to sleep. But he knew he must. Slowing his thoughts led to a recollection of that neither-here-nor-now place and that in turn led to light slumber which led to a full sleep.

Despite the happy occasion Peter Pan had more nightmares, terrorized by his perception of pirates, of failure at his lessons and of being alone on a savage island. And then the laugh came back. A terrible laugh that chilled him. It sounded familiar and yet distant. It sounded like an invitation to a fight. He tossed and turned.

When just enough light had cracked over the horizon to cast the world in twilight, a little white light dashed over to Peter Pan's tree. He still lay curled up by the trunk, his leg still arched. Queen Mab whispered in his ear, relieved that this little action woke the boy. She waited while he rubbed the sleep out of his eyes and let the laugh echo out. He eagerly followed Queen Mab (who remained silent) around the Path that had Made Itself, to the edge of the Serpentine.

"Loo loo! Right on time!" clapped Clark. "Now, Peter, before you say anything, I know what it is you're going to ask. All in good time. Right now, Clovis is expecting you. Loo! Follow the path on the right. You'll find him soon enough."

Peter shrugged his shoulders and began to walk toward the dirt and moss path. Queen Mab started to follow him, but Clark called out.

"No no, your highness. Loo loo! Peter Pan is to go alone."

She stopped in midair and watched Peter turn, for he heard what Chauncer said.

A short while ago he might have been very nervous going off into the woods by himself. But now he'd not have it any other way and with that he ran out of sight into the trees.

Queen Mab could not help but feel teary, much like a mother whose child requests to walk to school alone. She had to admit to herself that she would truly miss the troublesome boy.

Chauncer also looked on, admiring the toddler's self-assurance. He happened to know this quality pleased Clovis. Clark turned to his huge book and began scribbling the details.

Peter followed the winding path never once feeling scared despite the sights along the way. He encountered spikes protruding from the ground with hideous masks hanging from them. He tried to speak with a man before he got close enough to see he expected the attention of just a straw-filled dummy. He even passed a skeleton. He had never seen a skeleton but besides the obvious shape, he grasped his forearm firmly and felt the bone so he deduced the gruesome truth. If child-sized the loss probably would have upset him. But as this skeleton looked too large to be a boy, it merely tickled his curiosity and he stood over the collection of bones, fascinated.

Peter heard a thud and looked toward it. Not too far away stood a stone tower and its great wooden door had heaved open, slammed flat against the cold rock. A large intimidating figure approached, wearing a helmet resembling the Corinthian style (the sort with a bar protruding down over the nose, pointed teardrop openings for the eyes and blinder-like protrusions near the neck wrapping around toward the mouth). The helmet also had bat-like wings decorating the sides. Horns emerged from the eyebrows. The helmet brought darkness to his face and only the soft shine of white eyes could be seen. Around his body a V-shaped crimson cloth covered his chain mail. He wore high boots and metal-plated legs. Two swords were sheathed on either side and a midnight blue cloak trailed behind.

When the armored figure came within earshot, Peter stanced himself. "I venture you are Clovis. I am Peter Pan."

Clovis remained still.

Peter wondered at this. "Well? Get on with it."

For many moments more, Clovis stayed motionless and when he finally spoke his voice sounded like a bear talking in a tin can. "Follow." He turned sharply, clinking as he went and Peter Pan followed.

They traveled deep into the forest but Peter soon recognized the area they moved through. They passed that little home and before long they came to the oval arena. Peter trailed Clovis all the way into the center of it.

In one graceful swoop, Clovis unclasped his cloak, tossed it aside and unsheathed the two swords. Peter watched with delight. "I shall," said Clovis, "surmise your current level of expertise."

"Oh," said Peter matter-of-factly. He didn't know what Clovis meant, but he pretended that he did so that he could grasp the sword all the sooner.

"From your size and the experiences you have had above, I suspect you to be at a certain level but we shall see how you fare. Put fear aside. I shall not harm you. Just do what comes naturally for you as you try to fend me off. Begin." As the word 'begin' resounded from his helmet, he tossed the smaller of the two swords at Peter.

Peter reacted quickly and caught the sword by the handle with ease.

Clovis's eyes shone for a second. "Impressive, Pan." But he did not wait to thrust his sword forward and the blade pierced Peter's belly, running him through. He froze, unable to shake off the daze from the cruel action. And while he remained like a sitting duck, Clovis stabbed again and just as before it merely stung a bit with the pain subsiding as the sword withdrew. "Concentrate, Pan."

Peter gripped the sword tighter and jumped back. He examined his belly. No damage at all. Clovis lunged again and

Peter reacted. His blade came crashing against the other blade and forced it down. Clovis swung it back around the other way, but Peter parried this one as well. Two more quick and different maneuvers from Clovis were pushed away by Pan with ease. But then, not fast enough, he received a cut on his arm. In the throes of fighting, he did not freeze as the invisible wound stung and went away. Then Peter leapt up to avoid a low-cutting swing. He pushed down a few more thrusts. To avoid a slash, Peter moved to behind the teacher, but Clovis suddenly darted his sword behind himself, scraping across Peter's legs. The whack sensation came and went. He backed away.

Clovis turned around. "Very good, Peter Pan."

"You hit me some of the times!" he sulked.

"Ah, but you fended me off with surprising style. You already prove yourself to be way beyond Egidio."

"What is Egidio?"

"The beginning level meaning kid, or young goat. But you are moving rapidly toward the next." As he said this last part, he charged at Peter without warning.

Peter doubled around in a circle and stabbed Clovis in the back in the same manner as when his own legs got slashed.

"Bravo!" Clovis exclaimed, still attacking.

Peter came to see how much he had craved this kind of activity. His heart raced and he loved it to do so. The fight became more than an activity, it turned to a game. He leapt out of Clovis's new attack and pierced him at the same time. Peter then lunged forward himself, leaping high into the air. He aimed his blade downward and cut right into his mentor's side. Peter parried the next two blows like they hadn't happened at all and then whisked his sword around with such vigor that Clovis had to parry *him*.

Peter's flurry of prowess, though brought on by his own volition, perhaps had some unknown help. Someone had wandered into the arena unseen. He sat down on the edge and watched. It's possible that the rooting for Peter Pan by the spectator boosted Pan's confidence. Either way, Peter had become a force with which to be reckoned whirling and gashing the sword in a deadly ballet. Clovis could not keep up.

As Peter forced him backward, Clovis called out, "By thunder! A blazing blade of fury!"

Pan held his short sword in the air, cried out in a kind of battle cry and bounded up toward Clovis. But Clovis whipped his sword and stabbed Peter in the air. Peter whumped to the ground. The landing hurt ever so much more than the sword gash. Peter lay there, panting.

Clovis twirled his sword around and stuck it into the ground. He walked over and extended a hand to help Peter up. As Peter dusted off, Clovis praised him. "Peter Pan, you surprise me! You have performed with grace and force. I dare say you move even beyond the level of Harbin, the little bright warrior. You dabble in the art of swordplay like you've always been meant to be doing it! I have no choice but to station you at Caddock, the eagerness for war. All in all, bravo! I have not seen the like of such natural and quick progress!"

"Oh?" said Peter, ignoring the compliments as if he knew he deserved them. "What about Jake? I have heard tale of how skilled he can be."

Clovis laughed good-naturedly and at the same time Peter heard a playful gasp from somewhere not too far off. Pan turned his head. There, near an orange flapping flag, sat none other than Jake. Clovis waved him over. He had known all the while of the boy's presence.

The moment had come at last! Not waiting for Jake to move, Peter did instead, throwing down his sword, jumping half of the way over and running the other half. Peter's enthusiasm startled Jake a bit. Pan stood in front of him, looking. Jake had a matching set of crimson pants and coat that appeared to be made of the same material as Clovis's garment.

Jake broke the silence. "Hullo, Peter." Peter had not yet found his voice. "They tell me that you have been asking about me ever since that night we met."

Peter's voice returned with a rant. "Oh, I have. I have wanted nothing more than to play at games with a real boy for such a long time. Children don't get to stay behind in the Gardens very often and even then not many boys, but then came you. And you wanted to stay with me, Jake! No one ever stays with me. And then –"

"Then I got taken away."

"Yes."

"I have thought about you often, too, Peter." Jake gave him a smile. "I wondered why you did not come down and have lessons with us. Now I know it's because you are a natural talent. I have been watching you fight."

"Oh what fun it is!"

"Peter, do me the honor of sparring with me."

Playing something adventurous with a real boy!

As they walked together, Peter thought to ask, "What level has Clovis given you, Jake?"

"I'm a Kincai, battle leader. That's just one level shy of the final one," Jake said with pride. He caught Peter's twinge of feeling inadequate so he added, "I have been studying for a long time. Clovis's lessons are my favorite in the Drowned Forest."

"I can be a Kincai. Just you wait!" Peter said sternly.

"Don't worry, Kincai is just above Caddock. Besides, Clovis says that no one has ever reached the last level."

"Then I shall be the first!" declared Peter.

They stopped in front of Clovis. The Combat Master pulled his sword from the ground and handed it to Jake. Peter darted to one side and reclasped his sword.

"Begin!" Clovis rang out.

Stab! Jake pierced Peter's shoulder. Peter growled lightheartedly and stabbed back. But Jake went quicker, moving backward out of reach. Peter stamped his foot and moved back himself. Jake waved his sword tauntingly. Peter swung his sword upward, two fisted, summoning the power he just had in his last battle. A mighty whoosh followed and Jake dodged this as well but Peter whisked around in a rapid spinning toward Jake who received a double chest wound. "Ha!" said Peter.

Jake and Peter had at it for a good many parries and jumps and swings and cross-stepping, each not able to get the better of the other. But eventually Peter got in that one quick blow that floored his faux foe. This move did not daunt Jake, who made a wondrous backward jab at Peter even before the quick shooting pain went away. Peter felt his own pain and jumped back. Jake turned around and they began another series of sword clangs, fending each other off.

Then Jake's sword made a speedy swish and double back maneuver, managing to hit both sides of Peter's ribcage. Peter ran away for a bit, but not out of fright or defeat. Jake chased him, which is what he wanted. Peter looked back and saw that Jake had a good momentum. Peter halted abruptly and jutted his sword behind him, impaling Jake. He swooked the sword back out again and Jake reeled for a few seconds. As Peter stood smugly and gloated to himself, Jake hacked at his legs. Peter dropped from the fleeting pain. Jake rushed at him, sword aloft, but Peter expected this attack and with one hand he returned the favor. Jake joined him on the ground.

The two friends laughed together. They had tired themselves out and were glad when Clovis announced, "Enough!" The two boys stood up, still giggling. As they dusted themselves off Jake said, "Good match, Peter. Good match indeed."

Peter grabbed the hand that his friend put out for him.

"It's nice to spar against a real opponent," said Jake. "I've grown tired of the other boys. They're just so...so Harbin."

"Both of you are accomplished fighters," said Clovis. "I believe that is all for now. Go, have fun." He moved to the swords and thrust them back into the sheaths by his side. His armor clinked against itself as he trotted to his cloak and refastened it. He walked away, but called out, "Until again, Peter Pan. Return when I call. You shall hear."

"Ay," he replied.

The tower door slammed shut.

"So what do you do for fun, Jake?"

"Oh, things like tag, marbles, statues, King of the Hill, you know."

"No, I do not know."

"You don't know how to play?" Jake asked dumbfounded. "Even tag?"

"How would I? I had no one to play with."

"My my."

"Do you have any hoops here? I used to sail my hoop."

"*Sail* your hoop?"

Pan sighed. "So Maimie had been right. She told me I played the wrong way at them. I do not see her anymore. And she no longer writes letters to me." He caught himself feeling sad, for it is quite sad, especially since he could no longer read them if she had, but he decided it neither the time nor the place for sorrow. "Jake, can you show me how to play at hoops?"

"Would that I could. There are no hoops in this Forest, nor do I really know how."

"How peculiar. I thought all boys could do hoops."

"No. But I know as much as that they do not go in the water." He paused, then said, "I don't feel much like playing. Our battle tuckered me out. Let's just sit on the grass, have some berries and talk."

Willing to do anything as long as his friend did it with him, Peter said, "If you like."

They asked about each other's worlds, since they each knew very little about the one in which they did not live. Aside from the varieties in their companions, their lives seemed very similar. They both frolicked a lot of the time. And each had schooling of sorts. Rather than combat or Nature lessons, Peter learned the grand manner by the fairies and had great success with his personal experiments on his pipes. Jake showed great interest in the pipes of Pan, for Peter told how he could play Nature, such as a branch shaking. Jake vaguely recalled hearing them that fateful night in the Gardens. While they talked, Jake gathered some of the berries he promised. Arone had taught not only which ones were edible but how to select the ripest ones. Peter ate his share greedily, for he never tasted such sweetness.

Do not think for a moment that Peter Pan didn't come around to telling Jake how he would soon be in the Neverland. The news really caught Jake's attention. He begged Peter to be allowed to go with him.

"But of course. And we shall never leave each other's side. Except when we do."

"Surely."

"I should warn you," Peter said. "Great dangers are in the Neverland. Wild animals, people with red skin, pirates..."

"Sounds all the more grand!"

"I think so, too. Have you ever met a pirate?"

"No. Just my parents. But they're not pirates. Or I don't think so. I don't remember them well. None of the boys down here much remember their parents."

"Me neither. I don't know any pirates. But when I meet one, I shall stand right up to him!" Peter declared.

"How do you know so much about this island?"

"The fairies told me. And Sylvanus said –"

Jake stood up. "You have met Sylvanus!?"

"Sure. You have not?"

"No one gets in to see Sylvanus. How did you do it?"

"Oh. Well, I am Peter Pan." The little boy who did not want to grow up said this with such conviction and authority that Jake cut himself short in asking what it meant.

At Jake's behest, Peter stood up and followed him. They did not go terribly far into the woods before they came to a round clearing of sand. A rock jutted out at a near forty-five degree angle. Climbing the slab, Jake beckoned for Peter. They looked out over the expanse of the Drowned Forest in silence for a little while, both of their little heads filled with thoughts of wonders awaiting them in the Neverland.

Then the tin can bear voice echoed in Peter's head. Clovis, of course, called him back.

"I believe Clovis calls me," said Peter. When he looked at Jake it became obvious that the same thing happened to him.

"Ah, yes, well, Arone is calling me. I have advanced lessons today."

They walked toward their respective destinations not thinking much of the goodbye, as they hardly knew it to be one.

The moment Peter arrived near Clovis's stone tower the door swung open. Peter entered and climbed the winding stairs to a sparse tower room. A treasure chest lay pushed up against the wall and some weaponry hung on the walls. Other than these things, it merely had a rough stone surface.

Much to Peter's dismay, this lesson had no fun sword twanging, rather a sword haranguing of history and terminology. Clovis spoke at length about the annals of swords, information both dull and sharp. The dull became too much for Peter Pan who only partly paid attention as he didn't see why he had to know such things. But soon Clovis steered the lesson to the terms and stratagem. Pan perked up for this part, newly eager as he came to realize that swordplay had more than just swinging the blade around. Artful maneuvers in hand to hand combat, swordplay and strategy abound and all of it the sort of rough and tumble that excites a boy.

Finally, Clovis instructed Pan to return home. He must spend the night in the Gardens and resume his lessons the next day. Clovis led him down the steps.

"How do I return without help from Queen Mab?"

"Nickert is on his way for you at this very moment. He shall return for you at dawn and bring you back into the Drowned Forest."

"Ah, so I get to meet this Nickert at last." Just as Peter finished talking, the door of the tower slammed behind him.

A distorted cloud of grey appeared suddenly. "Allo." The blurriness took shape. Peter could now see Nickert in his true form. The little grey fellow had an over exaggerated under bite and pointed ears. These matched his pointed tail. His legs curved a bit so that he seemed perpetually falling forward. Rounded horn stubs adorned his head. Nickert looked friendlier than the definition of the word will allow. He appeared as the cutest little devil.

"You've given me quite the stirs, Nickert," Peter said.

"Never my intent, young one," replied the little grey devilite. "Merely doing my duty. Very sorry to have caused you alarms."

"Oh, that's okay. I'm over it now."

"Ready to return to the Gardens?"

"No." Peter said. "And I don't see why I must."

"Ah, that. Well. Don't worry, lad. You'll return. But until then, I'll tell you what I think. I suspect something wonderful will happen when you get back to the Gardens."

"You do?"

"I do. Now, ready to depart?"

"I supp–" he began, but could not finish the thought, whisked away before he knew what happened. Peter had the sensation of damp waves of air rapidly zooming past his face. He could not see anything except many smudges. Then it all settled into reality and he found himself in front of the tree in Kensington Gardens he called home. Peter turned sharply, but Nickert proved nowhere to be found.

Colandrion sat in the tree's hole. "Welcome back, Peter!"

"Hullo."

"Queen Mab is expecting you. We better go."

"So soon?"

With that, Colandrion zipped away and Peter followed.

Chapter 6

Huitzili

The Queen had ordered the greatest possible fanfare and the very best decorations to be set up where Peter Pan had landed when he first arrived in the Gardens that evening of evenings. Colandrion flew over the Serpentine and Peter relished that he could swim across with ease, even if some swans did provide a bit of help, repaying his kindness of giving them his day's food in the past.

Never had such adornment been displayed in the Gardens, which is saying a great deal owing to the amount of gala events of late. Peter could see the festive grounds and markings from far away. Queen Mab, seated in the most splendid of thrones and dressed bedazzlingly in a gown resplendent with dewdrops, could barely stop herself from fluttering over and her glow seemed brighter. But she managed to maintain a solemn countenance — a rather tricky feat for a fairy, and only Queen Mab had mastered it.

Instinctually, Peter bent down on one knee and bowed.

"The reports from the Drowned Forest say that you are moving along well, Peter Pan. You have met your end of the bargain with flying colors which leaves me no choice but to hold up my promise as well. Thus, we gather at this ceremonious occasion to restore something to you." She clapped her hands.

A large portion of winged fairies zipped out of the throng and darted toward Peter's back. Immediately they tickled him on the shoulders, sprinkling dust just as fairies had long ago. Peter felt the familiar itching.

Flight at last! The fairies expected that Peter would not be able to refrain from scooting through the air all around the Gardens. And they were correct. He swooped up and down, in circles and figure eights. He sailed low and high. Peter waved at the birds still up at this hour. The wind rushing by Peter felt so delicious that he did not ever want to stop. But he knew that he must, so he forced himself to land back in front of the Queen. His crooked grin proved gratitude enough for Mab.

"We have another surprise for you, Peter Pan." She clapped her hands and a parade of gnomes came from out of a tree, with four of them holding up a package wrapped in leaves. Not until they come close did it become clear that the parcel had not been surrounded by leaves to hide it but had actually been the gift itself. "May we, wonderful boy?" asked one of the gnomes.

"May you what?"

"When we heard tale of the boys you know having little outfits, the prospect of stitching together a suit seemed to suit us just fine. We have taken it upon ourselves to design an outfit for you. May we help you with it on?"

Their tailoring measured nothing short of exquisite

He nodded, thinking of the nightshirt he used to have which has been long since gone as a sail and nesting material. In a flurry of activity with just a little difficulty (solved by a gnome standing atop another) the leaves began to cover the boy. Their tailoring measured nothing short of exquisite, but some parts did not quite meet all the way around. Fortunately quick thinking and cleverness prevailed and cobwebs did the trick. These silky patches also adorned the suit, adding a sheen that all admired and they knew the job to be complete.

Then the party commenced. They all drank, ate, danced and romped themselves silly. The goat got into some of the cowslip wine and hobbled around in a pleasant stupor. And this night the fairies had a special treat for Peter. So that he could enjoy this, most likely the last of the special events in his honor, the fairies put together an orchestra. Their instruments ran the gamut of ingenuity such as humming into grass blades, strumming on stems, beating on stones, using the tambourine some child must have left behind and blowing triumphantly through hollowed out twigs. They had a beautiful, full sound that delighted Peter. He remained hovering just above the ground simply because he could. Such a grand affair it turned out to be. The supply of Wall-flower juice nearly depleted due to the number of wee folk who needed refreshed from all the dancing. They stayed out very nearly up to the opening of the

Gardens! Then Peter felt damp, heard a whoosh and a blurred vision came into focus.

Peter laughed, "You sure do come and go quickly."

Nickert replied, "I can only do so when fetching or delivering boys. And the farther away from the Drowned Forest I roam, the more my power wanes. Thus, it makes it difficult to avoid detection."

"You mean people might catch sight of you?"

"Surely. But I have learned to be cautious and can pretty much stay out of sight. People have a tendency to ignore the obvious, I've found."

"But how glorious the feeling of living on the verge of danger must be!"

"I'm glad you think so. There have been glimpses of me. My having to rest or recharge in water has generated a few stories about me. Unfortunately they are unflattering. Misunderstood is the delicacy and care of what I do. And what people do not understand, they all too often assume to be wicked. But come, Peter Pan. Clovis expects you."

"Oh well, if I must," Peter said with a smirk of joy.

They waved to Clark as they passed. He nodded, said "Loo!" and chronicled their entry.

When they reached the stadium, Peter saw all of the boys of the Drowned Forest. Clovis stood in the center of the arena.

Peter moved over to him, walking. He knew better than to take flight right away. He stood a few feet from the master. There were no words exchanged. Clovis tossed Peter a sword and they fell to it.

Peter Pan did not disappoint his spectators at least insomuch that he put on a good show. A couple of the boys were disappointed that after very few lessons Peter showed more promise than themselves. How did he do it? A deadly dance. Clovis could barely believe it himself. Peter Pan had somehow become more skilled than the prior day. The master could not even get in a scratch on the lad.

Clovis gave a great cry and one of the boys came running, sword in hand. Now Peter Pan had to fend off two opponents. This boy, even though he had just been bestowed Caddock status as well, proved no match for Pan. Peter simply focused on the fun of it. He thought back to his talk with Nickert. To always stand at the precipice of danger. Having lived such a placid life, he loved the idea of potentially being wounded, savoring the curious thrill, giving him the sharp focus he needed. He moved always one or more steps ahead of his sparring partners.

Clovis grappled with more than just his sword and his opponent, torn between becoming angry with Peter Pan for being so hard to hit and parrying every blow or filling with exhilaration for his astonishing pupil's success. Another war cry, another boy leapt into the ring.

For a time, Peter held his own against the three rivals. But then Clovis gashed Peter. Even before the quick sting of the cut subsided, Peter returned the blow to Clovis and brought down the new boy. Pan relished every second.

Clovis called again. Four opponents vied to get Pan, but he jumped about and whisked his weapon with a dazzling fluidity. His rivals were thrust back no matter how many times they attacked. If the great battle trainer Clovis had not been experiencing it for himself he would have punished the one who described such a scene for telling egregious lies.

Now there were just two challengers, the original Caddock boy and Clovis. The other two were reeling from exhaustion and thinking they could somehow still feel the stings.

"By thunder!" said Clovis. He now gave a shrill whistle that resembled the battle cry. The boys on the ground leapt up and Jake and another boy in the sidelines rushed into the stadium.

And then, the formidable onslaught of six adversaries began to prove too much for Pan the lad. He received several slashes but kept fighting, even though forced to lose ground. But then something happened.

Losing ground is precisely what Peter did. He leapt up and remained in the air. A whole new set of aerial maneuvers took place and he zipped about, darting forward and back and to and fro and here and there and then no! there he...wait! no! here he comes! Whoosh! Stab! Flip! Parry! Spin! Attack! Dash! Slash! Zip! Touch ground, thrust.

"THUNDERATION!" shouted Clovis as he sat up from the ground. All around him his boys lay about moaning. Peter stood tall and proud, twirling his sword. Then Peter leapt into the air and crowed. He floated gently to the ground and bowed.

Clovis yelled out, "HUITZILI!"

At this word, Jake sat up. "What!?" he exclaimed in a strange combination of joy, disgust, jealousy and disbelief. He thought he would never hear the word from Clovis again. He stood up and passed by a boy dusting off his crimson pants. "Clovis, you can't mean it!"

"Ay. I can and I do mean precisely what I uttered."

"What is Huitzili?" asked Peter.

Jake answered. "The last status level, Peter. It is only for those who behave like a hummingbird."

Clovis continued, "Ay, Pan. Huitzili is an honor that I have not bestowed before. In all honesty, I made up that level of achievement in the belief that it could not *be* achieved. I used it merely as motivation for my students. But you have proved me wrong." Clovis got on one knee. "Praise to you, Peter Pan, for showing me the meaning of my own creation. Hail to the Huitzili Warrior, Peter Pan!"

The other boys were still in shock, but they bowed.

"But Clovis, isn't flying cheating?" asked one of the boys.

"One makes use of whatever advantages and skills one has," came the reply.

All the boys talked at once, bombarding Peter with questions about how he flew and fought like that. The leaf-clad lad had only one response after he waved his arms to quiet them.

"I am Peter Pan."

Jake had of course heard this before, but this time it actually meant something! Obviously whoever this Peter Pan happened to be, he should not be crossed. Thus, out of some fear, some respect and some thirst for adventure all the boys vowed allegiance to Peter. Surely having him on their side would behoove them. After a round of cheers from the boys for Pan, Clovis spoke to Peter.

"I cannot teach you further, Peter Pan. Oh surely I could teach you more of the proper terms for the moves. I could show you more appropriate stances, explain more history. But given that you can flit about like a hummingbird, such things become moot to a little boy. Besides, I doubt you care for them. Congratulations, Peter Pan, on being the one and only Huitzili."

More cheers.

"Go now. Play with your fellows until Arone calls you. We are done here."

His cloak about faced and before long they heard the great door to his stone tower shut.

"If you will remain on the ground and not cheat by flying, then we can play tag," said one of the boys.

"What is tag?" asked Pan.

The other boys laughed, except for Jake. He shushed them. Higgins explained to them Peter's situation of having no one to teach him such games. He reprimanded them for their callousness. Could any of them play the sounds of Nature on bundled reeds? Could any of them fly? Were they master swordplayers? The taunting ceased rather quickly.

Peter soon learned the easy game and they had a long and involved round. They moved to a large knoll within the forest not too far away and taught Peter the game King of the Hill. He played very hard at this one and became undefeatable.

Eventually, Arone's reverberating call let Peter know that his leisure had to come to an end. He followed the pseudo-humming to that little mossy home in the woods. The dog-headed, one-legged fellow greeted him by an open door.

Would that what transpired within the home of Arone could be delineated. But the teachings of this great Nature

Master must be kept secret. Suffice to say that Peter received an earful of useful and artful information about plants that can be used for medicine, the principles of roots, shelter building, food gathering and the like. Peter showed interest, as it seemed akin to the juice remedies of Solomon's Seals and Wall-flower used by the fairies of the Gardens. Pan asked many questions, but most importantly of all he asked Arone about the nature of aging. Yet even he could not answer Peter's riddling eternal youth of old.

And thus went the education of Peter Pan in the Drowned Forest of the Serpentine in Kensington Gardens.

Chapter 7

Flight

Peter Pan spent just a few more nights in Kensington Gardens. The fairies were too reluctant to let him go. But one night when a nearly full moon hung low in the sky, casting an ethereal glow across the London park, Peter saw something that urged him into haste. Dancing playfully to the fairy orchestra, he came very close to the Round Pond. Peter Pan could not believe the reflection staring back at him in the moonlight and would have fallen in with a great splash if some fairies had not quickly come to his aid and pushed him back up. Of course it had to be himself, but the rippling image did not look like him at all. Yet it did not lie. How he had grown! To call him a tot could hardly still be accurate.

"Stop!" he cried out to the crowd of fairies and animals. "I say! Stop the party!"

With some grumbles, the festivities dwindled.

Peter continued, "I must leave!"

"But the party!"

"Fie on the party! I saw myself in the water. I am a big little boy. Still young, I dare say, but ever so large!" He examined the cobwebs of his outfit and how over-stretched they seemed. His apprehension mounted in his voice as he said, "I cannot stay here. I must go to the Neverland!"

Colandrion flew over. "You shall be going soon."

"Right now!" Peter crossed his long legs and hovered.

"You shall go," Queen Mab said, zipping over. "But it cannot be right this minute."

"Right this minute!" Peter repeated.

"But Peter Pan, we cannot take you to the Never-Never Land ourselves. Our cousins who reside there must send The Fairy Council to come get you."

"Then summon this Fairy Council. I am to go to the Neverland now."

"What of the other boys? What of Jake?" called Colandrion as he rose higher toward his friend.

"I shall have to come back for them. It is no use me taking them now. I shall scout it first," decreed Peter Pan. He pointed at Mab. "Summon the fairies."

Fearing he might become even more demanding or cross, the Queen signaled to some of her attendants in the know. They rushed off. "Plan on going when the moon is full," said Mab.

"It's full enough!" yelled Peter.

"Hush, boy! Do not forget that we are not above mischiefing you."

"You wouldn't dare," he replied.

"You would make a lovely stone, you know," said the Queen. She knew perfectly well that she would not do this, for it has already been established that they would all too likely forget what they did to him. And if they did remember, who could say him to be this stone or that rock, especially if children strolling in the Gardens during the day found him and used him for this game or that one. Nevertheless, it proved a sufficient enough threat to keep Peter quiet.

The party mood dwindled in dancey so much that their attempt to start it up again failed even when the fairies picked up their instruments. So they cleared away the grand affair and all, except for Peter, went to bed with heavy hearts. He moved about in the Kensington Gardens in a melancholy, but never unhappy way. He stayed up late roaming, flying about and never realizing when, where or how he went to sleep. But he did know that in his sleep the piercing, terrible laugh followed him, stronger now than ever. It found him, even nestled in a hidden thicket of branches.

The next evening Colandrion flew in his ear. "It is time to go," he said sadly. Peter slept lightly, so the fairy fellow woke him with the words just before Lock-out Time.

As he followed the fairy, Peter pounded the side of his head gently, as one does with waterlogged ears, in an attempt to get the echoing laugh out of his head. When he stopped he noticed a group of seven fairies standing on the ground. Three of them were dressed in elaborate, ceremonious outfits made of a smooth, shiny material Pan had never seen before. The fashion of woven strands of polished leaf stem had not yet sprinkled over into the mainland. Those three fairies stood so as to make a triangle in front of the others. The remaining four, though they had ceremonial garb, did not have the shiny clothing. They stood in a square behind the triad. The forefront fairy, glowing bright mauve, spoke.

"Salutations, little boy," he said the way one speaks down to a child. "We are the current assembly of the Fairy Council in the Never-Never-Never Land."

"I just call it the Neverland."

The fairy grunted and sniffed, as he did not like being interrupted. "I am called Yorth. Behind me, you will find Kelana, Weaver, Plokon, Slena, Pitcher and Betin." Each fairy bowed or curtsied at his or her name.

"Hullo," said Peter.

"Have you made all necessary arrangements to ready yourself for departure?"

"I believe so." He turned to Colandrion. "Have I made all my arrangements?"

A nod, peppered with sadness, replied.

A few feet from the ground, Peter remembered something. "My goat!"

Colandrion flew up to him. "We shall take care in your stead. Besides, you will be coming back for the boys."

"Oh," said Peter, happy at the easy solution.

"Very well," Yorth said as he ascended. The others took his lead and motioned Peter to follow. Pan reached inside his tree and grabbed his pipes. "Well, then, goodbye for now, Colandrion!"

"Goodbye!" the fairy said with a tear wholly conspicuous in the corner of his eye. "Goodbye!" But Peter did not hear the second, more sorrowful farewell since he'd become a speck in the sky. But he could not have heard anyway over the clang of the bells from the Gardens. If anyone would have looked up from the bustle of exiting, they would have been treated to a wondrous sight.

It must be said, for it cannot be denied, that someone did see. A lass just knew she didn't pretend seeing a little boy flying away with some stars. And be sure that she told her friends, then one boy related it to legends of Peter Pan and so his story carries on, a fact which would please the boy to no end.

Peter fixed his gaze on the landscape both ahead of and below him, knowing unbounded delight in flight. He had flown outside the Gardens before, certainly, but many years had passed since then. As the landscape of London spanned underneath him, he felt glad indeed that he spent his life among Nature and not amid the angular, piercing architecture. Yet awe washed over the boy and the world appeared a refreshingly disturbing place. A charm all its own, Peter thought, especially as he and the fairies soared over Bloomsbury, a part of the city which looked perfectly lovely with the little patch of garden park at one of its corners.

In not so much time that could be readily noticed, the boy and the fairies passed beyond the borders of the famous English town. Now vast flat fields and bumpy terrain sprawled out to greet him. He wondered at these farmlands, wishing he could drop down and have a gander, but the fairies pressed on and he did not want to lose his way. Right when he first thought that he might, a little blue light came by his head. Pitcher spoke: "Let me tell you, boy, you must take heed and stock of your surroundings. Remember them well."

"All right," he said tersely, knowing he'd probably forget. But he really did try to imprint it on his mind, noting they had practically been following the Thames River.

Heading westward they flew and flew and still longer they flew. One of the buildings in the distance caught his eye. He spied Eton College, which made him shudder, for it looked exactly like the kind of place he figured he had evaded by flying out his window as a baby. A solemn quality hung about its stones, a distinct feeling of grown-ups and of growing up very fast. Peter Pan shuddered again and then just looked straight ahead. Later a sight came into a view more curious than any he had yet seen. It looked like giants had played at blocks. Although somewhat disheveled, he looked at a ring of rocks, standing upright. Many of the stones were topped with other rocks, creating little doorways.

Peter Pan descended, soaring toward the mighty stones with every intention of passing through each and every entrance between the thick pillars. The fairies quickly changed their course and each grabbed a bit of his hair, yanking him back toward the path.

Peter grumbled at their insolent gesture, but did not let go of his curiosity when they let go of his hair. "What on earth is that?" Peter asked eagerly.

This time Betin's mauve light flared next to him. "A very ancient arrangement. So ancient that the silly humans have forgotten its origins."

"Do fairies know?"

"Of course," came the reply.

Before Peter could say he needed to be told, the queer arrangement faded from view and Betin had already rejoined the other fairies. Peter watched as something that looked like the Serpentine but much, much bigger came into view. When they hovered over it, the fairies encircled Pan.

Slena said, "We have reached the ocean. From here on it behooves us to fly higher and consult the stars. Do you know how to do that?"

"Well, I've spoken to them and they have winked back."

"Ah," she continued. "Then you are halfway there. Trust your instincts and try to hear them. Winking is their language and after some practice you shall be able to talk with them. You'll find that if you can speak fairy, you will be able to pick up on star."

"Why should I need to?"

The fairy ring spun around him so that Weaver faced him. "The stars, silly boy, can be useful. Though they cannot take direct part, they have quite the influence on terrestrial affairs. You'll discover they will gladly help guide you to the Neverland." The wee people spun again and Plokon said, "You see, we have informed them of who you are and what purpose you serve. Thus, they shall let you know when you go astray."

Peter Pan flew onward with the Fairy Council

And so Peter Pan flew onward with the Fairy Council. They soared over the great ruggedness of Appalachia. Still onward they flew. And flew. And flew. He swore that he'd been flying so long that night had turned to day and become night again or had there been two bouts of darkness in a row? He never thought that he could tire of flying, but hadn't he been

119

flying dreadfully long? Pan had just begun to wonder at how much of the journey yet remained when Kelana whispered in his ear. "The other thing to note," she said, "is that the Neverland also now knows about you. It is looking for you more so than you are looking for it."

And then, there it loomed, at last! For anyone else, the Neverland comes into focus like eyes adjusting to darkness when a night-light suddenly goes out. But for Peter Pan, it all showed up at once in a kind of bang. Rapture burst inside him making his feet wriggle, his legs shake, his torso quiver and his arms fling open. He let out his loudest cry of joy yet and the crowing of Peter Pan blanketed the whole island. He had not imagined it so grand. Not waiting in the least for his fairy companions, he tore through the sky toward the rich, lush, gleaming and foreboding magic island.

"Impetuous youth!" grumbled Yorth, the only one in the Council who deemed the whole ordeal preposterous and unworkable.

Slena said, "Precisely what this place needs."

"Ay," agreed Pitcher, "an angelic devil to sort all this out!"

"Did any of you notice?" asked Weaver.

"Notice what?" asked Betin.

Weaver replied, "This boy we have brought...he saw the island all at once!"

"All at once!" repeated Plokon in disbelief.

"Holus-bolus!" exclaimed Pitcher.

"Well, that puts a new light on things," Yorth had to admit. "Perhaps Mab has not gone as daft as I believed."

"Well, he surely belongs here if he can see it all at once on first arrival!" clapped Plokon.

"Who knows what sorts of adventures he'll be able to muster and master if such a feat comes naturally to him!" Kelana exclaimed.

"Speaking of adventures," said Betin, "where is Peter Pan? Should we not find out what the boy has come upon?"

Chapter 8

Meetings

Peter Pan had made it all the way to the other side of the Neverland even before the fairies finished their conversation. He wondered how this section could be Winter when he had entered the isle in Spring. A magical place to be sure and he clapped with joy. He moved on, flying a bit lower now, soaking in all the strange whimsical beauty of the island, splashed with colorful sights. Not too far off in the distance rushed a great stream. But this stream flowed straight down! We have all seen waterfalls, of course. But imagine Peter Pan's reaction to seeing one for the first time. He dashed through the air toward the magnificent and shimmering falling water. Once close enough, the thunderous gushing both delighted and deafened him. But curiosity won out. He found himself fighting the downward current. But being able to fly enabled him to easily escape the downpour. He laughed. He heard more laughing. But not the sound from his dream. These were alluring giggles. He turned to look for the source. He soared off and finally saw, just over yonder, many ladies bathing in the water. He hovered gently down to introduce himself, alighting on a rock jutting up in the pocket of water, a long way from the base of the waterfall, surrounded by palms and grassy gnarled hills. "Pardon me, ladies, I do not mean to inter–"

But a sight cut him short. Large fish attacked the girls! He moved with quickness, but no farther than the edge of the rock and he saw the truth. These lovely ladies had long fish tails. He stared for some time. Their giggling picked up and Peter crept backward on the rock. He kneeled, staring, as he found he could do little else.

Bubbly giggles interspersed the following words: "Ola!" "Bonjour!" "Aloha!" "Ya su!" "Guten tag!" "Hej!" "Servus!" "Konishiwa!" "Hullo!" "Malia goe!" "Shalom!" "Hiya!"

Peter remarked to himself just how miraculous this place proved to be at every turn. Surely he would be happy here — adventure enough to keep a boy occupied at every moment. Meanwhile, the water ladies swam closer. He leaned toward the one nearest to him. "Hullo," the lad said. She made a smile that harbored both loveliness and wickedness.

"Come on in," she lulled, extending her hand. There seemed to be a spray of chorus sinking behind her words.

But Peter resisted her wiles. He shifted his position, coming to sit a bit farther back on the rock. The one that invited him sneered, leapt up and dove back into the water. She swam away in a huff. The others were about to do the same when Peter stretched out his hand.

"Wait, pretty water ladies!"

His words pleased most of them and their giggles intimated that flattery would do very nicely. They floated nearer to the rock.

"Please don't go," Peter requested.

"Give us reason to stay."

This threw Peter for a loop, for he had no idea how to please a lady, especially the sort who are part fish. He did not think, or even know, that he simply had to continue complimenting their exotic beauty to make them stay. Instead Peter Pan did what came naturally to him. He blew into his pipes. He improvised entrancing music such as they had never heard, nor were able to produce themselves. As a result, of course, the sea maidens could not help but stare at the boy clad in leaves on the rock. Those who had swam off came back to

124

listen, even the one who had first approached him, all of them mesmerized by the music of Peter Pan. He played on and on, very pleased to have an audience other than fairies and critters. His music drew to a crescendo and then the melodious sound rippled away. The ladies clapped, splashing and thrashing their tails to add to the applause. Peter had to move to avoid being hit with water.

Mesmerized by the music of Peter Pan

"Pray tell, little one," said the one who had wanted to dunk him, "who are you that you can summon sound so sweetly?"

He stood and bowed, just as the fairies taught him. "I am Peter Pan."

"Well, Peter Pan, you may play for us anytime you'd like," said one with red hair.

"Stay with us," said another with a sea shell sash.

"Oh, surely. I intend to stay. Except when I go."

"NO! You mustn't go!" said yet another with a starfish on her black locks. Her tone seeped ominously into the air, changing the brightness of the lagoon.

"No, I really must. But I shall always come back." After an eerie silence, Peter spoke again. "Please tell me who or what you are."

A splash of chuckles erupted. "Mermaids, you silly boy," said still another who dared get closer. She had an awful look in her eye. Peter had seen the look in fairies about to mischief. He flew up out of the way when she tried to grab him. "You cannot catch me!"

A round of gasps.

"What a wonderful boy!" remarked the only mermaid who could muster her voice at the sight of a hovering leafed piper child.

From the air he fluted some more and the maidens of the sea sank into the music. To their intense dismay, he lost interest in playing, quite suddenly, in mid-note.

"Thank you, mermaids," he said. "Now if you'll excuse me, I've got some exploring to do, so I shall be away."

This comment met with sounds of discontent, but the boy ignored them and zipped away into the clouds. And thus, the mermaids forever want more of Peter Pan.

He continued touring the island from the air, and every time he happened to pass along a particular route again, he swore another nook he'd not seen at first dash had cropped up here or there. He raced toward some smoke rising from an encampment that looked like tiny mountains. But as he came close, the smoke got in his eyes and he changed course. Contentment in soaring above it all quickly became a craving to be among it all. Peter Pan launched like a cannonball then backflipped in midair, pounding his feet onto the sand of the isle's shores.

Now just footprints could be seen, for the boy had already darted his way into a lush jungle. He brushed aside brambles, crawled under overgrown roots and swung on vines. Somewhere along the way the jungle eased into more of a forest. He liked having so many trees around. In Kensington Gardens the trees bunched together, but a path always stayed close at hand at one turn or another, if not a whole open field. Here in the Neverland a deep forest surrounded him and he relished being right in the midst of it. It took no special skill to detect and sense the danger that lurked about. And presently just yonder stood a pack of wolves with thick, matted fur and bared teeth, their yellowed eyes narrowing as the growling began. A terror before him, a real danger the child of the Gardens had never imagined. Steadily they sauntered toward the boy.

At a venture, Peter turned, then bent himself so as to look at them through his legs. It didn't happen in a moment, but quickly afterward the wolves dropped their tails and fled.

His deed didn't go unnoticed. Yorth the fairy zipped down to Peter Pan. "Remarkable, boy! Absolutely ripping!"

Peter shrugged. "It just seemed the thing to do."

The rest of the Council had caught up, both to the actual spot and also regarding the scenario. When they heard about Pan defying the wolves so easily by his own design, each of them had to admit the lad had proven himself as the missing piece of their mystical land.

"Do you have any questions?" Pitcher asked Pan.

"Where are the pirates?"

"There are none on the island just now, boy," answered Betin. "And I can tell you: they will not confuse so easily as the wolves."

Peter Pan changed the topic. "Do the Redskins live in big pointy things?"

Slena tinkled a laugh. "Indeed."

"Well, then, I shall pay them a visit." He launched himself into the sky.

He already knew the way back to the Redskin camp and flew lower to avoid the smoky air. He didn't think about the fact that he had not been invited and landed conspicuously out in the open, right alongside the very large cooking pot hung over an open fire wherein the evening soup bubbled.

Peter folded his arms and many braves sprang up — some with a stretched bow, others with a tomahawk, a few with knives in the shapes of birds and still others curling their fingers. "Hullo. I am Peter Pan!"

Not impressed, the Redskin warriors closed in toward him.

Peter reached for a sword, but found he had none. His movement set the archers to twang and Pan leapt out of the way of the arrows. With no weapon he didn't stand a chance, for he doubted very much he could charm burly men with a melody. So he bounded over them, alighting atop their totem pole. The disrespect for their tribal symbol doubled the internal growling of the Redskins. But not all of them looked on with anger.

Peter would very much have liked to know that he had an audience, but alas, he'd been too wrapped up in his own antics to notice the coquettish figure amid the bramble. The young maiden stared in wonder. A pale skin, free as a bird, yet terrestrial all the same, with no thunder in his heart like the men from the sea. She felt lighter, unable to keep her bearings. Waiting moments longer than would have been respectable, she returned to her wigwam. Her mind churned, upset by the disrespect of the pale boy and yet thrilled by his actions.

More arrows let loose at Pan. He soared out of the way, stayed in the air and scratched his head as to why they shot at him when he'd done them no harm that he could see. Such unfriendly behavior! He thought their reputation as savages correct while ducking a spear.

"You don't have to be rude!" Peter Pan told them not realizing that he'd been quite rude himself on many past occasions. He shifted his position to avoid a flying hammer. The brave who threw it dropped to all fours and Peter could not help but wonder at the dangling silky strands attached to red-crusted ovals that hung all about him. Pan ultimately had to swoop in for a closer look, narrowly escaping not only another spear hurled at him but the lunge of the brave on all fours.

Peter Pan flew up and out of range. He had enough of the Redskin camp. Surely he could find someplace else on the island that would prove less hostile. But such a task proved easier thought than done. True to the isle's reputation, much lurked about which did not seem any more friendly than the Redskins, whether a bear or a tiger or an ugly and disgruntled overgrown telluric fairy who belongs under a stone bridge over the river. Not that Peter Pan didn't pester any of them, for he became increasingly amused by the game of evading capture.

But when not engaged in an encounter, he enjoyed many delights ranging from flowers unlike any in the Gardens to refreshing streams. He flew about the island, circling it with the careless loveliness of a sea-gull.

The Fairy Council found him sprawled on the bank of Mysterious River.

"Well, Pan, do you find the Never-Never Land suits you?"

The lad tucked his hands behind his head, as if this answered Yorth's question.

"We're impressed with how you handle yourself here," said Plokon.

Peter arched his leg.

"You already know your way around," observed Weaver.

He wriggled a bit, like someone desperately trying to become comfortable.

"Do the perils worry you and thus keep you quiet, wonderful boy?" Kelana asked.

Pan took a deep breath and exhaled just as deeply.

"I'd say he rather seems as though he enjoys being in harm's way," Pitcher commented.

A wicked grin.

"Such an expression on such a sweet face!" gasped Slena.

The impishness increased and he rolled to his side, holding up his head.

Betin demanded, "Enough silence, boy! Tell us what you are thinking!"

Peter sprang up, set his legs apart and said, like he truly believed it, "I am home."

At precisely the moment he finished his words it seemed like a tidal wave crashed over the whole of the Neverland. The fairies felt the effect just as much as Peter Pan, who had already disappeared into the sky. Their mauve, white and blue lights chased after him. Peter now realized that some of the sparkling bits here and there across the land had to be fairies skipping about. The Neverland teemed with the wee folk in a way in which Kensington Gardens could only aspire, even though the number of fairies who inhabit London's expansive park amounts to no paltry sum.

When the Fairy Council tracked him down next, Pan held tight to the horn of a rhinoceros, his legs kicking and swaying gaily over the brawny beast (with a little help from his power of flight.) They gaped fearfully at the boy's body jerking to and fro, but he rode with no shortage of laughter and cheers. The rhino's temper flared up with a speed to match its legs. At top velocity, it crashed into a hollow log which easily lodged its way onto the horn, and Peter Pan had already deftly reached a branch of the tree from which the log had fallen. Some common street fairies watched the shenanigans, marveling even more than the Council. Peter Pan did take note of his audience this time and sweepingly bowed, crowing with all his might.

Without warning he dashed among the glows of the Fairy Council and he said, "I am ready to go back now."

"When you are having so much fun?" Plokon countered.

"Ever so much!" he exclaimed. "But I could have more fun with my friends. And if I am to face the pirates and these other bigger nasty-looking fairy folk and such, then I'll need a suitable weapon. I bet Clovis has one for me. Take me back to Kensington Gardens!" he smiled brightly.

"A few of us will accompany you, but you shall have to try and find the way on your own," Yorth said.

Peter nodded confidently. Arms stretched out ahead of himself, he soared away from his miraculous playground. At first he did not have any trouble, able to follow the reverse route with ease. But even before he came to the western shores, he felt more than a bit uncertain of the way. Plokon, Betin and Slena watched his hesitation. When he'd hovered in one place, searching for his direction for far too long, Slena flew up to his ear and whispered, "Do not forget whom you can ask for help."

In a twinkling, Pan did recall and shot straight upward.

"Stars! O stars! Show me the way back to London."

The largest of the stars in the Milky Way screamed out, "Follow!"

A few of the lights in the sky shone on and off in sequence, making a trail. Soon enough, somewhere over the Grand Canyon, Pan called back to them, "Very well, I have it now!" With that the blinking stream of stars stopped. He whisked himself all the way back across the other sea with dazzling aerial acrobatics and the journey went by quickly. Peter Pan alighted on Bird Island, thinking how small it now seemed.

Chapter 9

Adventure!

Peter Pan returned to Kensington Gardens with joy in his heart like never before. He skipped about, all the recent sadness forgotten. But immense joy must wane eventually and this joy would fizzle in not so short a while. Even though he mostly heard Sylvanus, he should have listened a bit more. He would not have imagined his new life so carefree. For now, Peter Pan fluted a merry tune and gathered up a large audience. A throng of Garden creatures, even the finches, squealed at his return.

Thaddeus Crow hopped all the way across a branch and leaned over at the tip toward the boy. While Pan took a break from blowing the sounds of rapture from his flute, the crow called out, "Why, Peter Pan! Did you have a good escapade?"

"I did, yes! And I shall have more."

Thaddeus cocked his head. "My, how you've grown, dear boy!"

"Oh, pooh!" he grumbled, then stomping his feet at each word said, "I really don't want to do that!"

"Do the fairies reckon you will cease to grow again?"

"They seem to think so. But they are so flighty. Mayhap they are just fluttering their words about to keep me quiet."

"Play!" cried a fairy in mossy pants climbing up to a mushroom and wishing he had wings to zip at Peter's face to complain further about the lack of music.

"No," replied Peter. He flew off in search of his goat.

The fairies, especially the street sort, began to sorely regret the restoration of his power of flight. But even though many of them had held secret meetings as to how to ensnare the boy and keep him forever among them, they knew the plan to be a futile one. They had to face the truth: The boy had outgrown Kensington Gardens. Very undancey indeed!

As extra luck would have it, being dancey prevailed just the night before. It's no great wonder, of course, since the fairies can find one excuse or another for a fancy party at the drop of a petal. So without a doubt, as they are wont to do, a fresh fairy ring sprouted up on Bird Island. And the reason a fairy ring could be considered even luckier than usual becomes clear as Peter Pan returned gliding alongside his goat.

"My goat will come with me to the Neverland. I demand it done," Peter announced while crossing his arms. He looked severe, confident and so much larger (and not just in stature) than the fairies were used to seeing him. Moving amid the waking dreams of the Neverland had already changed the boy and they could only say for the better, as far as they could tell, before switching to a feeling of trepid awe.

"Easy enough to arrange," winked a blue fairy.

Peter heard Colandrion. "Do you remember, Peter Pan, a girl named Maimie Mannering?"

"At times. I just mentioned her to Jake." He pet the goat with one hand and gripped a horn playfully with the other.

"As I know the story," Colandrion said, moving in no great hurry toward Peter, "she brought out the goat from her imagination. She'd do so at night to frighten her brother, who believed in the goat, all of which had been done in the moments of falling asleep." Peter nodded, thinking he should. "Surely you know it's magical. How else could the goat have survived with you lo these many years?"

"I suspected so," said Peter convincingly. "Maimie left a letter asking you fairies to make it real, and you did."

"Precisely. Now step into the fairy ring," instructed Colandrion.

Peter moved his long legs into the mushroom circle.

"To save your goat seems the plan,
What do you ask, Peter Pan?"

To which the youth replied,
"I ask you to cast it far and wide
So in the Neverland I may ride."

He then flung his arms about as if he sowed seed, and turned around three times.

Next Colandrion said,
"We shall send the goat far from here
To adventures of both joy and fear."

And Peter answered,
"By dark and light I fondly swear
The Neverland we both will share."

The goat disappeared, but Peter could vaguely hear it bleating. Of course it had been a mere trifle for the fairies to relegate the product of the imagination back as such and this way Peter could keep the goat in mind on his trip back.

"Just tell the island fairies to return the goat to you."

He had but a moment to enjoy the ease of solving the transport of his goat before a watery dash of grey swept him up and transported him just as quickly as the goat vanished.

"Loo Loo! Hullo again!"

Gathered behind Clark Chauncer stood Arone, Clovis and Nickert, who just scooted into place next to the others, with Queen Mab hovering between the two teachers. "Sylvanus is waiting for you," she said.

Once again Peter Pan made the trek to the keep of the old master woodsman. Due to great assistance by flying, the journey did not take even a third as long. They even let him lead the way. Before him towered the gigantic gate once more. Still not touching the ground since his arrival in the Drowned Forest, Peter grabbed hold of the massive door and pulled with all his might. When he could fit, he flew inside. He did not expect the spindly woodsman to be standing behind the column-tree with his arms stretched wide.

"Salvere Jubere, Peter Pan, Guardian of the Neverland!"

Peter Pan bowed.

"Guardian?" echoed Queen Mab.

The boy looked up at him with gleaming eyes.

Sylvanus spoke with all the intensity and sharpness of a beam of sunlight. "You have heard how exceedingly well this boy has done on all accounts on the island. Has not the Fairy Council long searched for someone to tend to the Never-Never-Never Land? He's the answer to many a prayer."

"Please don't fill him with any more delusions of grandeur," said Queen Mab.

Cicadas chirped for the laugh of Sylvanus.

"Pan, you have earned the right to not just live in the Neverland, but to be its caretaker as well." Peter Pan stood proud, feeling quite important indeed. "And for your efforts, we shall grant your request."

Although one would not think it would be so, it is precisely this moment which squelched the joy out of Peter's imaginations of his adventures-to-be. For although Sylvanus triumphantly announced "Behold, the Lost Boys!" only two came trotting out from behind the curtains of leaves.

"Where is Jake?" demanded Pan.

"Loo! Forgive me for not already saying so…loo loo! Jake will be late. That is, he'll be here soon. He's having a lie down for the moment. Took a big shock a while back, he did."

"Worry not, dear boy, he is fine!" Sylvanus assured him, tousling Peter Pan's abundant hair with his thin and gnarled fingers. "But here! Greet those who are to be your playmates."

The two boys stood on either side of the enchanted woodsman, almost close enough to feel the fur of his legs on their cheeks. Peter recognized them both and he liked each of them well enough. "Why are there only two? Last time I played with as many boys as printed on the bank-note I once found in the Gardens!"

Clark's hands touched Peter's shoulders. "Loo! Back they went, you know! Claimed, before their seven days' time, you see? Just these two are left! Loo!"

He could not hide his sour disposition. The two boys joined him in a long face, for they, too, missed the other boys, but, behaving like fairies, they could not remain sad for very long when real fun awaited so close.

Peter looked them up and down. "I'm captain," he said.

"We know," they said in unison.

One of the boys had red hair, complemented by his soiled crimson jacket, and his naturally wide eyes darted all about.

"What are you looking for?" Peter asked him.

"I just like it here. Not so crowded with trees like most of the Drowned Forest."

"In the Neverland, there are plenty of woods and overgrowth," Pan boasted as if he'd planted them himself.

"I would prefer the open space."

Peter shook his head. "I lived in an open space, more or less, all my life. You just wait. You'll love the dark forest. It's full of wild animals."

The boy gulped. "I think I'd much prefer parks."

"I'm ready, Captain Pan!" the other boy said, sounding brave. He had dark, nearly black hair and his shoulders were as plump as a proper sausage. Unlike the other boy, his red coat did not have a single mark on it.

"First," said Pan, turning to Clovis, "I need weaponry."

"Ah, but Peter Pan," said the tin can bear voice, "you will find my artillery does not survive outside the Drowned Forest. And even if it could, it would do your opponents no harm. For be ye warned, boys, the graces of your fights in my arena are not so in the battles of the Neverland. There you shall wound and experience pain. You must take your skills to heart if you wish to survive."

The boys swallowed and had a look at their captain. Pan did not flinch, wearing that same austere look on his face as when he called for his goat to be attended to, looking fiercer now than before. "How shall we defend ourselves without arms?"

"Can you not think of any way to obtain the weapons you desire?" asked the strategist.

Pan rubbed his chin. Adventure still coursing through him, an answer came to him rather quickly. "Lost boys, do not fear. I have a plan for a load of fun we shall have very soon."

The boys thrust their arms upward and cheered.

"What's all the fuss?" came a voice. Jake Mortimer Higgins popped out from a curtain of vines and grass.

"Jake!" exclaimed Peter. He bounded across the air and landed with his arm across his best friend's back, giving a slap. "Let's fly!" He shot up in the air, but heard grumbling so loud it grounded him. "Whatever is the matter? Don't you trust me?"

"It is not that, Peter Pan," said Jake. "You are the huitzili, not us."

Peter half-spat in admonishment of the thought. "I can teach you. You just lift yourself up," he said, demonstrating how.

All three boys jumped up and came down immediately.

"I say," said the redhead, "how do you stay up?"

"Queen Mab will soon have you flying."

"Very big of you," said the Queen. Even though her words sounded sarcastic, the truth is Peter's willingness struck the fairy with shock – to share part of what made him special! But she didn't think like a little boy. Of course he needed his friends to fly so as to have all the more fun with them. And what's more, in order to reach the fabled island of deadly playfulness, they would have to fly.

"Though you will not fly so well as me," Peter Pan said.

"We'll arrange it in Kensington Gardens," Mab sighed.

Sylvanus gave each of the boys a pat on the back and without a single word or whistle, filled them up with abiding comfort. Clovis saluted. The boys returned the gesture. Peter Pan gave a nod. Arone hopped up and down on his leg, both eager and sad to see them all leave. "Loo Loo! Goodbye, boys!" said Clark. "Whatever you do now is up to you... my books shall be marked up to the moment you leave, but your exploits thereafter are thine own!"

"Ready?" Nickert toothed out with his underbite.

The Lost Boys, not wanting to admit their apprehension, each nodded along with Captain Pan.

In a few whirs the little grey imp had all four boys on Bird Island. Jake came last and he lost his balance, falling into the dark-haired lad who dropped into the dirt.

The redhead looked about. "It *is* open spaces!" he cheered.

"No," said Peter Pan. "This is my old home, the Kensington Gardens. What is your name?" He didn't seem to mind the sudden switch in topics.

Still relishing the landscape, the boy said, "I like parks!"

"Parx is a funny name. But it will do," said Peter.

"But my name is –"

"Parx," said Peter, narrowing his eyes.

Parx decided not to object. Besides, he found he couldn't remember his name anyway.

Peter, ready to tell the fairies to rekindle their wings, looked about and saw he had to go fetch the other boy who had trotted over to the Serpentine. Pan watched with curiosity as the boy scooped up water and rubbed his arm with it. He looked, then scrubbed again, all too determined to wash away the dirt.

"Why are you doing that?" Pan scolded.

"I just want to be clean."

"Washing? When fun awaits? See how Jake is at the ready!" He pointed to the blonde haired lad, standing akimbo. "Rubadub, indeed!" Peter chuckled, then looked around for the queen. "Jake, Parx and Rubadub need to fly."

Queen Mab called forth a number of fairies and the shoulder tickling began in a jiffy. Peter Pan took off, not allowing any time for pleasantries, reminiscing or explanations. Jake already soared up toward Pan. Parx and Rubadub shared a look then launched themselves into the joy of flying.

Just as Peter imagined, the boys did not fare so well at flight, lacking the experience to master maneuvers that came naturally to him. But they made the trip nevertheless, wobbly though they may have been against the sky.

No fairy came along to guide them. Pan did not need any help at all. He moved from view of the boys frequently, giving them a stir. But Peter always came back to the head like a leader in a flock of geese. The boys sank now and then and had to keep flapping their arms (which Parx swore helped quite a bit.) Their captain shook his head at them mockingly and just kept saying "Like this!" and then flying ever so softly and swiftly.

Before long their flapping slowed down because they spent so much of their time bumping into clouds and staring down at the tracts of land and giant pools.

On and on they flew, amused by Pan's acrobatics. Peter had really only been trying to amuse himself and the boys quickly lost interest in trying to emulate him when they nearly teetered right out of the very sky. After too much time, they had to open their mouths to complain of the trip.

"I think we've been flying forever," said Parx. "It's too much open space. Even for me. What do you think, Rubadub? Do you think we've been flying forever?"

"Ever so much forever," Rubadub said, brushing off a bit of cloud. "Do you think we've been flying forever, Jake?"

"I say, it does seem very much like –"

Peter halted suddenly. He pointed. "There it is, boys. The Neverland."

Unlike Peter Pan, each lad saw a form on the ocean hazing into focus. Bits took shape here and there with colors aflame. A happy sigh resounded from them all at the sight of the true make-believe island.

Parx and Rubadub cheered, their arms pushing even more skyward and rushed toward the isle. Peter Pan let them go, smiling at their squeals of delight. But Jake moved slowly. Not for want of participating. He even tried Parx's flapping again, but it soon became a clawing through the air. Peter Pan flew to him. "What's the matter?"

"It's difficult to fly here."

"No, it's not." Peter darted about, encircled Jake twice and swirled back to his face all in less than a moment or so. "See? And Parx and Rubadub don't have any trouble." He added, snidely, "Although they might find trouble down there." He shouted their names and the boys began an ascent. Peter turned back to Jake. The boy still moved as if he reacted to gusts of wind pushing him away.

"NO!" Pan cried out, dropping like a stone in flight shouting at the island. "No! You cannot keep him from me! I will not allow my friends to be shut out!" He raced back up to Jake and began pounding on the air in front of him. "Let him in!" Peter Pan could not think of whom he meant to address with his yelling, but Jake suddenly found it a bit easier to fly forward and finally could zip about without a care in the world.

"What happened up there, Captain?" asked Rubadub.

"I cannot say," Peter Pan answered. Then, after an awkward moment, he leapt up and spun around to face them. "Who's game for adventure?"

"I am!" said Parx.

"I am!" said Rubadub.

"Most game!" said Jake.

Peter led them to the Redskin encampment, which lit up their awestruck faces even more than the sights along the way. Pan kept them at a safe distance amid the trees on the outskirts of the clearing. He knew his band would need weapons if they would spar with the Redskins.

"I wanted you to see the enemy first," Pan said.

"Looks like fun!" grinned Jake.

Peter stayed him with his arm. "Theirs is a genuine battle, boys. You should have seen the fuss they made when I landed on the big pole of funny faces!"

"At least it's a clearing," Parx smiled, hoping to summon his courage.

"Shall we see about those weapons, then, Captain?" Rubadub suggested.

"We shall," replied Peter with a grin as devilish as they come. "Onward!"

The Lost Boys of the Neverland chased him almost as fast.

He flew toward the shore and saw precisely what he expected to see, although he could not really have known what to expect. His experience with sea vessels had only been his overgrown nest, Shelley's bank-note boat and papers twisted into the shape of a boat that reach his island after dark, hoops and a toy he once found in the Gardens left overnight by a careless girl, who breathed a sigh of relief the next morning to see that Peter

Pan had saved it for her. She told everyone she met that glorious morning whether they wanted to hear about her good fortune or not. But at any rate, what drifted gently up and down on the water could have been absolutely nothing but a ship. "The pirates are here, boys!" he cheered.

The three hovered behind him, not wanting to admit being fearful.

"What happens now?" asked Jake.

Peter told them, "This is the first I have seen of the pirates. So I don't know how dangerous they may be. But I do have my plan." He remained quiet, studying the elaborate floating home.

"This is the first I have seen of the pirates."

"Tell us the plan," said Rubadub.

"We're to swoop down and surprise them. They would never imagine boys to attack from the air. We shall always glide just out of their reach — it's ever so much fun — and then we shall flit through the ship until we find their weapons and take what we want!"

"That's stealing!" protested Parx.

"Pirates are thieves themselves," said Peter. "So they deserve to be treated the same way. It's only fair."

"But are you sure we'll be able to avoid the pirates?"

"I can do it just by myself if you're too scared, Rubadub."

Jake chimed in, "Not me! I am not scared. I want to play!" His left fist thrust into the air.

"Then let us go!" Peter grinned.

Rubadub and Parx exchanged another look. Each knew the other wondered at Jake's recklessness, but even more so at the brash behavior of Peter Pan. Their glance couldn't last long lest they lag behind, so they flew into what they reckoned would be a heap of danger.

The pirates, it must be pointed out, did not have any distinctive reputations other than their personal delusions. No buccaneer legends walked these decks. Just another nefarious seafaring crew seeking refuge in the world. Now whom they just sailed away and now sought refuge from – that's another story.

When Peter Pan crowed the Lost Boys descended upon the burly and scraggly pirates. Would that they could have seen the funny expressions on each other's faces, but all eyes bulged at the little boys diving from above.

Finally one with a blue bandana tied around his head turned to look at the bottle in his hand. "You break into the special ale, Wilkens?" He spoke of the load of spirits they'd gone to great lengths and taken considerable risk to pilfer off the deck of a pirate so fearsome they say the Sea Cook would have buckled at his sight. This same cadaverous seafarer had pilfered the ale himself, right from the decks of the Queen Anne's Revenge some years back. The pirates swore only to drink the prized brew on special occasions, not just to savor the liquid treasure, but due to the potency of the punch. Wilkens merely rubbed his ruddy nose in reply and the aerial urchins now came just a few feet from the pirates' heads. Even though he knew the Revenge ale barrels to be intact, Wilkens fancied he might as well have been drinking it. He wiped his brow, thinking now that heatstroke brought forth the unusual vision.

Many of the pirates concocted a scenario in which they might be hallucinating, whether it be from lack of sleep or bleary eyes from scrubbing decks, but all had to face the very real moment of four young boys whooping around, waving their arms and calling like birds, circling, floating and dashing away without ever touching the wooden planks of the ship.

Peter and his band moved safely down the flight of stairs to the lower decks, since the pirates could do little more than scratch their heads. "Well now we know Skylights didn't tell no tales. This island *is* spooked!" said one with a shiny and thick belt buckle that matched the gold hoops in his ears.

Three rooms comprised of wooden planks over, and then down a hatch in the aft of the ship, Peter Pan touched the deck of the armory. Rack after rack of metal death lined the walls. Pan clutched the handle of a cutlass and swished it about. The weight and feel of it pleased him, much better than weapons of Clovis. "Grab a sword, boys!" The Lost Boys didn't need to be told twice, jumping at the chance to play with sharp, shiny objects. When they turned around to stab, the pirates had just entered the room and jumped back.

"Easy now, lads," said the blue bandana pirate, waving his hands so as to soothe them. "We don't wants no trouble now. We's just –"

"I am Peter Pan." The proud boy stepped forward. "Stand down, pirates," he said, mimicking the man's gesture. "Let us pass, taking whatever weapons we please." His expression changed to heartless jocularity.

Again the pirates stood dumbfounded, not knowing whether to laugh or run in terror.

Their small assailant made the decision for them, lunging into the air with the cutlass held high. The buccaneers scooched aside, then quick as a whip plucked rapiers, boarding axes and cutlasses off the wall holders.

Peter Pan's sword clanged hard against the mighty stance of a pirate sword and deftly swiped it into a parry position in another direction just in the nick of time. The blue bandana on the pirate's head rose a bit along with his thick blonde eyebrows, unable to fathom what diabolic force confronted him.

Thus began the battle. Steel clashed, footwork became fancy and tempers rose. Of course the boys had the benefit of bird-like power which meant quick jerks out of the way, just as Peter told them. It also allowed them to quickly and easily move the fight to another location. Before long, the boys of the air versus men of the sea reached the main deck.

The pirates soon learned not to surround Parx who did not take to having his space encroached upon and spun in wild fury with blade at length whenever they tried. Rubadub kicked pirates' shins when they approached. It proved ever so effective, but not as much as aiming for their faces. Naturally the buccaneers were not used to such ways. A hindrance but not necessarily a disadvantage, they returned the foul fighting techniques, flexing their mighty muscle.

Jake boldly and fiercely kept up, but probably would have done better if he had not furtively looked over at Peter now and then for a pointer or two. Out of the corner of his eye, Peter saw Jake tying to imitate him. Overall, Pan thought the boys lacked the skill he had seen in them before. But amid the clinking and twangs, he had little time to worry about much but his own skin.

What a marvelous battle — the likes of which the world had never seen! And neither side could say (nor cared to admit) which of them tuckered out first, but all would agree that the moment came when it just didn't seem like sense to continue any longer. Though each side would give a very different account as to what constituted sense. As far as the boys were concerned, they craved another adventure. Surely clashing swords with the pirates couldn't be all for a boy to do in the Neverland. Besides, Pan promised them a Redskin battle. The pirates, however, wished to be released of the burden of shamefully gaining no ground against mere boys – nay, bewitched boys!

So the first pirate encounter came to an end when Peter Pan flew up to the waving black flag, and with a dagger he'd picked up during the melee, cut it down with flying force. The Lost Boys had already joined him. The flag fluttered down, covering the pirates like the big dark cloud that formed in each of their minds.

Peter Pan and the Lost Boys laughed across the sky.

"What a game!" said Peter Pan.

"Quite that!" said Jake.

Parx and Rubadub smiled, for despite their better judgment, even they enjoyed themselves. "Look at this great sword!" Rubadub said, holding up his prize. Not that any of them knew, but it closely resembled a scimitar and its leaning backward shape pleased the boys and therefore earned it the undisputed distinction of 'great.' They kept right on showing off the rest of their spoils. A weapon filled each of their hands, which amounted to four cutlasses, the dagger, a cavalry sword, a boarding axe and Rubadub's scimitar. But for all their focus on sword sparring, they never bothered to see (nor did they have a chance to see) what else the pirates had up their sleeves.

The band of boys didn't waste any time before they descended upon the Redskin camp from above. And the Redskins stayed at the ready ever since Pan made his exit. A cry out in their native tongue alarmed not just Pan and his crew, but alerted the whole of the camp that the Boy of the Woods had returned. Every flap of every teepee flupped open and a throng of braves stepped into action.

The boys came upon them in a swoop that eased into running on the ground, right into the thick of the men with darker skin. The men were skilled with their weapons and as fierce as the animals whose hides they wore. The boys faced a fighting style altogether different from what they knew. The Redskins had shields, to name just one of their advantages. Round, painted and studded with bone and feathers, the shields batted away many swings of the boys. Peter Pan held his own against the enemy, pleased with how well his dagger handled in close combat.

If not for the boys' ability to flit out of the way, hideous scenes like the one presently would have befallen more frequently. The razor beak of a weapon in the shape of bird's head scraped a deep red line in Rubadub's arm. At the same moment, Peter Pan bashed down on the skull of a brave using a Redskin club.

A voice cried out a single word in utmost disgust. Peter Pan and the Lost Boys did not know the word, but they had no doubt of what it meant. It needed no translation. The fighting stopped, tomahawks lowered along with cutlasses and shields, until all weapons dropped to the ground. All eyes turned to the vision of beauty at the edge of the battlefield.

A lass stepped into the crowd, glowing without a shine and silently commanded a path through the combatants. She stopped at the cauldron, turned with a quick jerk – the fringe on her tunic and boots swaying – and crossed her arms. She spoke in her native tongue with her fellow men and women of the tribe. They held a discussion in solemn tones. The girl by the cauldron no doubt took charge and seemed to be winning the argument. They had not yet finished when Peter Pan cried out, "I do not understand. Can you speak bird?"

"Tiger Lily," she said, clapping her palm to her chest. "Talked tribe. Used coming age princess right to say battle fate. No like fighting wondrous foe. Marvel at flying boys." As she said this, she took note of how much bigger Peter Pan seemed than just the last time she saw him. Surely a great magic surrounded him if he'd been able to grow so fast. If only she had known such a fact would have upset him greatly. On the other hand, he'd delight to know that despite herself, Tiger Lily could scarcely help but be won over by his charming face. "You wield powerful magic. For that reason, let you go."

Peter Pan, who had enough of fighting the Redskins for now, bowed with all the gallantry taught to him by the fairies.

Tiger Lily ceremoniously nodded her head.

Peter shot a look to the boys, and they all picked up their weapons. Rubadub had a bit of trouble moving quickly as his arm gash seethed with pain.

"Before boys go," Tiger Lily said, "you," (pointing directly at Peter Pan) "say *mea culpa* for dishonor." She had overheard the Englishmen who now inhabited their home on the mainland mutter *mea culpa* to themselves. It happened more frequently than she thought proper. Observing their countenance, she knew guilt consumed them and thus she learned the Latin term. She used the words exactly to their meaning, and what an astonishing effect it had when she did.

For a moment Peter Pan floated speechless, but then, tuned to the message of her words even if he didn't know them like she did, replied, "You want me to apologize? For what?"

"Peter Pan mock Piccaninny Tribe totem!"

"When I flew by the other day? Aww," he said, "I just had a little fun."

He could read the expression that settled upon her now, too. It brought new meaning to the term Redskin. She fumed. "Ignorance not excuse, but stands against first offense. Go."

The lad and his cohorts leapt up. Then Peter swerved in the air and scooped up a shield and a spear, laughing all the way.

"Beware, Peter Pan!" cried Tiger Lily into the sky, "Beware the Tribe!" Long before he'd become merely a speck in the blue, the Redskin Princess drooped her head and slowly followed the path cleared for her back to her wigwam.

"Beware, Peter Pan!" cried Tiger Lily into the sky

The boys landed in a clearing, much to Parx's delight. Now that Rubadub had come out of the commotion, he could pay full attention to his cut and he wailed, stopping only to plead for sympathy. Peter Pan wanted to pooh-pooh it at first, until he examined the deepness of the wound.

"Fetch the leaf that soothes," Peter Pan said, directly to Parx, looking him in the eyes.

"Come again?"

"Go!" commanded Pan.

"What do you mean the leaf that soothes?"

"You know, like the dog man told us."

"Dog man? The pirate with the red nose?" Parx asked.

"Enough silliness! Rubadub is hurt!"

Parx looked blankly at him.

"The dog man with one leg!" said Peter.

"I don't know what you mean either," said the other boy over a flaring of his wound.

Peter Pan leapt up a few feet in the air. "Jake? Do you?"

"I'm on it, Peter!" Jake ran off into the forest in search of the needed plant.

"Take off your shirt," Peter told Parx. The boy did as told. Peter then grabbed a cutlass and sliced at the garment, cutting a good bit off the bottom. He wrapped it around Rubadub's gash and pulled tightly. The boy winced.

Jake came back, landed and said, "I did not find it." He pursed his lips.

"Do you know what you are looking for?" asked Parx.

"Sure I do. But it's not around here. By the way the moss is growing on the trees, I suspect we'd have better luck by the shore. But I didn't want to be gone so long." He tried to make it sound as if he considered that they might worry if he took too long, but the truth be told he didn't want to be alone in the Neverland.

"Well, I'm glad one of us recalls the Drowned Forest."

"Is that a place in the Neverland?" asked Parx.

"No, dunderhead," said Jake. "The Drowned Forest." More blank stares answered. "Where we just came from? With Clark, Clovis, Arone… Sylvanus!"

Rubadub and Parx exchanged their signature glance, then shrugged at Peter and Jake.

Pan and Higgins shared a glance of their own. They had no explanation why the other two forgot, but if Peter Pan had remembered particular bits of information he had learned from the Drowned Forest himself, he might have been able to solve the mystery. But it didn't matter now. "We need to find that leaf!" declared Peter. He rose and the other boys moved upward along with him.

But Rubadub came down from his hover quite quickly. "The wound. It stings so! I don't think I can muster up flying right now."

"Very well," said Pan, floating back until his feet touched ground. "Then none of us shall fly. It will be a new game. No flying allowed. First one to fly loses!" So the band of boys gathered up the weapons and shield to set off on a land quest for the leaf that soothes a wound.

Along the way shadows of wild beasts passed in the background. The boys stared down an enormous, ugly telluric fairy. This hobgoblin stood two thirds of the way up a tree high and seemed content to go on its way once the staring contest became tiresome. A few pesky aerial fairies flit about, encircling them, and making a general nuisance of themselves. They did amuse Parx and Jake and their craziness pushed Rubadub's pain from his mind. But apart from these incidents, the boys did not encounter much to impede their progress. Sure enough, Jake spotted the thick heart-shaped leaf. He plucked one off and moved toward Rubadub.

"What are you going to do?" asked Rubadub, shirking back.

"You really don't remember?" Jake asked.

Rubadub shook his head.

"I'm just going to rub some of the sap from the inside of this leaf on your cut. It shall cleanse and heal it."

"Oh." He liked the idea of cleansing, so he allowed Jake to perform his tasks. A sudden intense pang evaporated like his Drowned Forest memories.

A clap of thunder.

Peter Pan crowed. He loved to watch thunderstorms. But the second boom did not sound like it came from the sky. And on this part of the island only sunny skies stretched overhead. The boys looked in the direction of the sound. The pirates! Five of them. The blue bandana and yellow eyebrows, the one with a golden buckle and hoops as well as Wilkens and two the boys had not seen before. Three had swords in their hands, but two of them did not. Instead, each of their fingers coiled tightly around curved brass objects. Peter did not have long to wonder about them before they spoke to him in their loud bang.

Either the buccaneers happened to be lousy shots, or they aimed to miss so as to put a scare in the lads. At least for the moment. Peter ran, but not from being scared. He ran to give himself more time to better assess what he faced. The boys had already forgotten they could fly, as the game went on for so long and had become quite routine.

But try as they may, they could not outrun the pirates. The men gained on them considerably. Perhaps it would have been easier if the fairies following them didn't swish by Peter's face every so often. Even more irritating, they wanted to have a chat with him. "Go away!" Pan said, batting the air at them. "Or else help us!"

"You've something on your mind, boy!" giggled an intensely glowing white light. "Let us take care of it!" a mauve shine said. Peter Pan felt a chill down his spine. A bleating caused him to turn around, whereupon he then ran backwards, slowing down as laughter took over.

His beloved goat had materialized from thin air in front of the pirates, butting into one of them in an indigo coat and causing him to drop his pistol. For the all the mad bucking and jumping around, the goat attacked them all at once. The men's priority soon became getting away from this menacing animal, which even dodged two of their precious bullets. They had no choice but retreat.

The goat attacked them all at once

"When we get on deck, we're telling the cap'n," said the one in the blue bandana to his shipmates, "we set sail!"

"Ay, Kempton. Mad goats from nowhere now?"

"Besides, the man we stole the ale from will surely be back," shuddered Torq.

"Let *him* deal with this wretched island and its little boys!" said Byford, smoothing out his indigo coat.

Too busy petting and patting the goat with many cheers, Peter Pan and the boys didn't hear any of their words.

"You say it's *your* goat, Peter?" asked Parx.

Pan nodded, beaming with pride that having his very own goat pleased the boys.

The fairies who recreated the goat waited around for a "thank you" but, never receiving one, harrumphed away. In Peter's defense, he'd been busy collecting the pistol and considering how the goat might be able to carry Rubadub. The goat obliged, so long as Peter's hand remained touching a horn. They filled their bellies along the way with some magnificent fruits. What a funny sight to see them attempting to shake the trees when they'd eaten all that fell on the ground, rather than just flying up to gather fresh ones. And so they walked, and each time Peter Pan saw a bird he did not know about hitherto from the Gardens, he bestowed a name on it. They walked ever onward into the forest, despite Parx's objections.

Chapter 10

Discoveries

Peter Pan and the Lost Boys stopped to rest, for their strained calves made it ever so difficult to continue wandering. Each of them had their backs to a tree and the goat grazed nearby. They kept their weapons within a few fingers' grasp on the chance that a bear or some other animal would stir and sniff around. They thought perhaps a bear had made his way toward them, but the rustling turned out to be a brownie strolling home. Peter watched her for a while and it divided his line of focus just enough for him to see out of the corner of his eye. He stood, walked a few steps, then rose into the air toward one of the trees.

"You lose!" said Parx, meaning of course that Pan had broken the no flying rule, which suddenly came to mind at seeing Pan levitate.

Peter turned his head. "The game ended when we stopped to rest. So it's okay to fly now. I did not lose." He sounded more distracted than authoritative, but his conviction came through in his tone. He placed his hand on the tree. A smirk grew on his face.

The Lost Boys then watched Peter Pan vanish as suddenly as the goat appeared earlier. Where could he have gone? Jake sprang up, tossing himself toward the bark that swallowed Peter Pan. And that, more or less, is an accurate description of what happened to the leaf-clad lad. To be precise, however, one has to look at the tree in the way Peter had. Like the hidden passageway hole in the Drowned Forest, the boy didn't see a solid tree like anyone else might have done. He could view a twinge of depth and recognized it as hollow, like the one he'd been sleeping in back in the Gardens. But unlike his last bed, this tree went all the way down. Thus, it most definitely seemed as though he'd been swallowed by bark.

"Peter!" shouted Jake into the tree, for having come close enough he could recognize the natural trick. "Peter Pan!" he called again.

An echoing crow filled the wooden tube and the lad burst out in triumph.

"There's a whole place in there!" he exclaimed. "I could fly around in the dark with very little to get in my way."

"Let me try!" said Jake, already climbing into the tree. But alas, Jake Higgins could not fit inside, let alone go down.

"Not again! Let him in," said Peter who, it is safe to say, would have launched himself into a screaming match with the mysterious forces if he did not first see another opening in a different tree. "There! Jake, you can try that tree!" He pointed.

Now that he knew what to look for, Jake saw the hollowness in the one he'd been leaning against earlier and flew back over. He dashed inside and fit quite well. But another alas, for he could not descend, not one little bit. "Draw in your breath," Peter told him. At once Jake dropped out of sight.

It can be easily guessed that Parx and Rubadub had an overwhelming urge to try it out for themselves. Parx flew to the tree in which Jake entered, but having ears that stick out much more than his friend, he just rattled around like a bottle cap stuffed into its bottle even when he drew in his breath, actually more so when he drew in his breath. He flitted out and tried the trunk Pan had used, but a third alas, for he could not zip downward in there either.

"Try that one," said Peter who realized that hidden hollowness afflicted many of the trees in this area. Sure enough, Parx went below.

It seems the thrill of taking such a ride dulled Rubadub's arm pain and he made his way to a tree. He tried all of them, even a couple more that Peter Pan spied for him. But the boy could barely fit, to say nothing of dropping down. Rubadub wanted to cry, but Peter Pan stopped him the instant he noticed a tear forming by saying, "Come here, Rubadub." The boy obeyed and Peter looked him up and down, then turned his attention to the trees. His gaze locked onto one of them and examined it up and down in the same way. Next Peter put his hands on Rubadub's plump shoulders and pushed until convinced they had lost a considerable amount of their shape. Rubadub gave it another go and whoosh, he went down.

The three boys wound up colliding into each other a few times in the dark of the great space below. And not very long after Rubadub shot down the tree Peter Pan heard them cry: "Get us out!" Flying up did not seem to work. Peter Pan leaned into the tree that fit him and shouted down instructions on how to get back up.

By the time the Lost Boys had located their place of origin in the pitch blackness and had mastered coming to the surface, Peter Pan had already gathered a ring of fairies around him who could not resist a dance.

Yes, Peter Pan still had his pipes with him. Despite his tumbling from one exploit to the next, he'd managed to hold onto his flute of reeds the whole time by looping a vine around them. He didn't remember when exactly he'd done it, but it came about from wanting them with him and not with him at the same time. He could not simply put them down as he could in the Gardens. He trusted the animals and birds and fairies there to treat them with reverence. But none of the Neverfolk had made any such promises. So he devised fastening them on his person with the vines and thought himself rather clever at the time, but soon forgot until he wanted to play his pipes again.

As Jake emerged, the music filled his ears and he wondered how the dulcetness could ever have escaped his memory. Any uneasiness Parx and Rubadub had about their leader drifted away with the song.

It had become the perfect shade of night in the sky. If not for the glow of the fairies they would barely have had any light at all. Peter Pan let the tune draw to a glorious conclusion, such that none could complain that he had not played long enough nor too much. The fairies applauded. Peter gladly listened to their chatter upon seeing the great boy for themselves, and he felt even more pleased than the fairies about himself being seen.

Peter said, "Fairies of this island, I want you to go under the ground by way of the trees."

"Surely!" said a lady, in a flustering flutter at being asked, and a few others trailed her.

"Parx. Jake. Gather up some branches, tinder and kindling," Pan commanded.

In very little time Peter Pan and the Lost Boys slipped down their trees into the large room under the ground, however now they saw the true splendor by fairy illumination. Short and bulky mushrooms of enchanting color sprouted up here and there, much more grand than any mushroom on the mainland. They accented the big bump in the center of the room, which rather seemed like a very big mushroom trying to poke through. Sections of the walls dented outward and very few bits poked inward. It might not have looked like much, but one must remember the roots showing overhead from the trees above. An ideal romper room to spend the night for any would-be explorer. In a little while the light dimmed. The fairies had gathered at an indentation in the wall, no smaller than a very tall hat box, and it clearly set them into a giddy mood which switched to jealousy for each one of them fancied living in the little apartment. Peter translated the fairy language for the boys a little while, hoping they'd pick up on it quickly. Soon enough they would learn much of what they say is just as inane as the conversation he now recited. Peter clapped his hands once. A blue fairy noticed and flew over.

"Keep all the house lit, will you?" he asked, almost nicely. "Until we get a fire going."

"Where shall the fireplace be, Peter?" asked Jake.

Pan swept his arm at the walls. "Any part of the room where you care to light it."

Parx and Rubadub watched Jake set to work with the materials, not realizing they, too, had been taught how to make it happen. A great amount of tinkling distracted them. Soon enough the Lost Boys knew it to be laughing. The room brightened along with their mood. "Silly!" cried one of the sillies, who dashed over and ignited Jake's pile. With that, the fairies all flew out, arguing over what sort of accoutrements and embellishments would best spruce up the recess in the wall.

Already the boys had become used to their new dwelling. The fire glow danced in Parx's red hair as he watched Jake whittling with the spear Peter had taken from the Redskins. Rubadub examined his wound, mindful of keeping dirt out of it but not because he knew of germs or infections. But they were not silent. Not at all. They chatted away about this or that and it is a good thing Peter Pan did not know their conversations were just as inane as those of the fairies. One bit, though, did not seem so absurd. Peter complained of the feathers attached to the Redskin shield. He plucked them off, increasing his anger each time. Surely, he thought, they had not lived among the birds nor asked their permission to use their precious plumage.

The evening wore on and the Lost Boys each nodded off, but first came great protestations of not being sleepy. Parx went to sleep first, rubbing his big eyes one too many times.

Peter Pan awoke when he dreamt of the same awful laughing filling his ears. He grabbed the dagger, made sure of his pipes and went up to the surface. He preferred the nightmares of the Neverland to his own. Once his eyes adjusted to the dark he noticed wisps of smoke and investigated immediately. He deduced that the smoke came from the fire in their home below. It could give their hiding spot away if left unchecked, but he did nothing about it right now other than vowing to protect the spot at all costs. Yet the vow did not prevent him from soon losing interest and wandering off. In his defense, it had not been merely carelessness but the sound of a voice asking, "Who?"

"I am Peter Pan," he said toward the sound.

"Whoo?"

"Peter Pan."

"Whooo?"

Peter alighted on the branch where the owl sat and its large eyes seemed larger upon seeing him. "I already told you. I am Peter Pan, the wonderful boy."

"Whoooo?" the owl asked again.

In frustration Peter screeched a bad note on his pipes, which woke up several other birds who all began chattering to him at once. He interrupted them, asking about the Redskin shields for he did so want to know if it bothered them as much as it did him. But the birds went right on tittering as if they didn't understand him. What puzzled him further is that in addition to the birds of the Neverland, some swallows happened to be visiting, and were among those chirping. Peter Pan could speak with swallows without any trouble before, but now one could be just as productive by breaking eggs and not making an omelette. He sank to the ground and put his head in his hands. He pretended he didn't hear his own sobs.

"Lost, boy?"

Peter Pan looked up and saw, for the first time in his long young life, the other end of the age spectrum. But as horrifying as the lady's wrinkles seemed to the lad, his eyes were drawn to her presence and especially her hooked nose. She wore a plain brown cloak with a hood draped over her head. Despite her features, she looked kindly. She leaned on a staff, but obviously not from frailty. "No," he replied. "I live here."

"I live here."

"Only a brave boy would call the Never-Never Land home," she said, her eyes twinkling with concern while her mouth wryly smiled.

"I am indeed a brave boy," Pan answered, standing tall.

"Such a big boy you are, too," she said in a way as to tempt his wrath.

Peter's head hung and watched his foot kick a few wood scraps. "I wish you would not have said that."

"Oh?" Her eyebrow arched. "Do you not want to be big?"

"I want to be a little boy. *Always.*"

As she looked at him, he did indeed appear littler and she noticed a pearly flash in his mouth when he spoke. "Do you not think you won't be?"

175

Peter did not know how to answer such a question. He sighed, more desperate now than angry about it. "I just know that as of late I have been getting bigger and I would very much like to stop. For as I am now seems a fine size to be."

She nodded slowly. "A fine size indeed." She smiled and told him, "Don't fret, for I can assure you that you are quite young. After all, you have not yet lost your baby teeth."

"Am I supposed to have –"

"Tut tut!" The staff banged the ground. "Do not invite the notion, boy! Keep such questions out of your mind." Relaxing out of the forward lean which she fell into when the walking stick came down, she continued, "Let us just say that many your size would have been losing baby teeth by now. But clearly you have them all, so I would say you are well on your way to halting your age."

Peter Pan lifted into the air without even realizing it. "Queen Mab says –"

Her eyebrows raised and her grip on her staff tightened. "Know Queen Mab, do you?"

"Yes," he said curtly as if to point out the foolishness of the question and then finished his thought, "Mab thinks the island's magic might keep me young, as if I'd just been dreamed up. Can it do that?"

She leaned into her staff with both hands now. "A difficult question. Trees and plants grow, I know that much." She licked her lips. "You'll find time does wear on in the Never-Never Land, though it's practically impossible to say when or how. Measured by suns and moons but time blinks by — each blink the size of an ocean. It's a foggy sort of time." After a deep breath she straightened up without taking either hand from her stick. "I know something else, too."

She paused, but not to taunt him with suspense, and fixed her gaze toward the ocean. "About the visitors," she finally said. "One man in particular has been coming for years." The far away surf seemed to wash the color from her face as she thought of him. "A great count of years. Yet he does not seem much older than when his dark boots first touched the shore." A brisk chill wind whipped up from the sea and she had to attend to her flapping cloak.

"A pirate?" asked Peter, fearlessly flying toward her through the cold air.

She straightened up. "What a delightful boy you are," she grinned. "A pirate to be sure. Rather handy with his weapon and his wit even sharper than his blade."

Peter touched ground again.

The old woman seemed lost in thought, and then said, "I suppose I must count myself among those who enjoy longevity while on this isle."

"So in the Neverland you never have to grow older?"

"A lovely thought to believe."

Peter Pan bowed to her. "Kind wrinkled lady, you have made me dancey again!"

"Glad to be of help." She banged the staff, then said, "Fare well, wonderful boy. Stay on your toes."

Peter rose to tippytoe by way of flight and winked.

With that, the very small old lady with the hooked nose turned and resumed her quest of gathering wood. Peter Pan didn't bother to ask who she might be. In wilds of the Neverland, she could be anyone. And it mattered very little to Peter Pan, so long as she did not attack him. Besides, she gave him the answer he wanted.

So why did he still not have complete faith in it? Skipping along as the trees gave way to a jungle, a dark thought came. To fulfill his wish must he be trapped on the island? Perhaps to always be a boy, he could not leave. But he had to leave from time to time, didn't he? If not to simply visit his fairy and animal friends in Kensington Gardens, then to fetch the boys who had fallen out of their prams. Perhaps if he would not stay so long in the mainland? It would not do. For Peter Pan, not growing up meant not growing up evermore, and by thunder, he would find a way.

"Whoooo!" called the same owl. The one to hear him this time looked back at those traveling with her. She wondered if Quiver Fish and Unmasked Raccoon understood what the old woman had said. Did she herself grasp the meaning of those words? The braves resumed sauntering toward their goal not realizing that her goal had already been reached. Secretly she had wanted to see the wonderfully terrible boy. And now she knew the nature of the island. If Pan did not want to be any bigger, than neither did she. For despite the rude injustice surrounding him, the coquette fell victim to his wiles. Is it any wonder? How extra charming he must have been, so freshly steeped in magic! But she could not dwell on his mystery. She brought up the rear and in a few paces her arrow saved Quiver Fish from a venomous snake.

Chapter 11

Misgivings

The next morning, Peter played the Fairy Reveille.

The three boys stretched and yawned.

"I say, are we still here?" said Parx, opening his wide eyes to the fire's embers still doing their best to keep a hearty glow.

"It's rather like waking up to a dream," said Jake.

Giving himself a once over as he sat up from his bed on the ground, Rubadub said, "I'm dirty." He then slapped himself in a minor frenzy, brushing off the earth.

"You'll just be untidy again, Rubadub," Peter told him. "We're setting to work at once."

"Work?" asked Jake.

"Our chimney leaks." He saw the wonder in them so he explained, "I went out last night and had all sorts of adventures." He lifted up his arm, proudly showing a scratch. "The smoke could lead nasty Neverfolk right to us. We shall have to make a disguise for it."

"Oh. Is that work?" asked Jake.

"I wouldn't know," Parx said. "Do you know, Rubadub?"

"I wouldn't know either. Peter Pan, do you –"

Their captain had already gone out of his tree.

After Peter showed them the spot that leaked smoke, each boy gave an opinion otherwise as to what should be done about it. They walked and floated around the area, scouring for a solution. Not until they took a rest did the answer come to them. Parx had lain himself across an overgrown mushroom. Overgrown, that is, for the mainland, but not for the Neverland. Peter Pan knocked on it. "This will do the trick," he said.

He grabbed a cutlass and whacked at the stem. The boys followed suit, until they realized both that Pan wanted to do it himself, as well as the painfully obvious fact that haphazardly hacking it would not be a suitable method to make a clean cut. Parx suggested they make a slice in each direction of the compass, saying he had a recollection of which way pointed north, and that the middle might be so ashamed of not being included it would leave in a huff. Rubadub, and it not even need be said, chose a path with the least ensoilment. But working at arm's length would be rather difficult. Jake wanted to heave it down, but that could break off too much of the stem. In the end they worked together to saw the mushroom close to the ground.

Even with flying it part of the way, the heftiness of it wore on them as they moved it slowly and carefully so as to keep it intact, for it had to appear like a mushroom belonged in the spot. Naught but a third of the distance to go, Peter Pan ordered them to put down the mushroom. He whipped out his dagger and began to core it, keeping a thick stem wall. A laborious task, but he enjoyed every last slice. The Lost Boys watched, a little glad not to be doing all the work yet wishing they could have done it themselves. When Peter finished they found lifting the mushroom all the easier. And when placed atop the chimney they admired the fungus of their labor.

Peter Pan clapped the dirt off of his hands with a look at Rubadub and said, "It seems nothing is really work unless you would rather be doing something else."

A pounding noise tumbled through the trees. Does it come as a surprise that Peter Pan soared away toward the source of the sound? He navigated over bushes, under brushes and through gnarled branches only to come back to the Redskin camp. The pounding came from their tom-toms and the rhythm almost played in time with a Fairy Reveille. Peter's brow crouched. Now he would scold them for their flagrant use of feathers.

He moved stealthily through the forest, savoring the moment of closing in on them, unaware that he moved in time to the drumming. Along he went, like a wild animal and when the tom-toms reached their climax and ceased, he burst out from some shrubs with a loud crow. "Redskins!" he called out, as if he could command their attention. He nearly alighted on the totem pole but saw Tiger Lily emerging from her teepee so he landed instead on a wicker chest. "How dare you!" he said. "Did you ask for the plucked feathers of my friends? For you see," he said proudly, "I am part bird. I cannot abide by –" But he could not finish avenging the avians for he spied the horn of an animal in the hand of a man. Peter Pan knew the ridges on that horn quite well. He moved his hand as if tightening it comfortably onto its curve. He flew down to the ground and advanced on the man, who stood adorned with many feathers himself. And then came another sight, transforming Pan's anger into sheer horror. He swooped backward into the sky for both a better look and to get away from it. An animal carcass roasted on a spit while some of the people whittled at hooves, polished bones and stirred juices in clay pots. Still more smoothed out the hide while others cleaned their carving implements.

"What have you done?" cried Peter Pan. "*Why* have you done it?" he said from the ground. He hadn't felt this betrayed since the conversation his parents had about him or else by Solomon Caw. Whichever of these hardly matters, since the unfairness stung him no less now.

The Redskins had butchered his beloved present from Maimie Mannering. It wouldn't help Pan to know the tribe had acknowledged the animal's sacrifice in sincere gratitude and its pelt and parts would be put to many good uses. Tiger Lily eased through the crowd but Peter Pan leapt into the air.

Flying back to his friends, he swept the horrifying scene aside but there always it lingered conspicuously in his mind like a bit of dust that shows up after sweeping the rest of the floor.

Jake saw the unpleasant expression on Peter's face and asked what had upset him.

"Nothing," Pan lied. "Let's get into some trouble."

"What made the booming sound, Peter?" asked Parx.

"The Redskins," he called back from the air.

The boys flew on after him. After playing the rest of the day away with half a hull of a long boat, having had quite the time with a mess of tangled vines and exploring a shallow cave not to mention other sundry games they found themselves in, including wrestling with lion cubs, the band of boys wound up at none other than the Mermaids' Lagoon. Pan's lads had not yet experienced the half-human maidens, but after witnessing the likes of the goony birds and trolls, such a sight did not surprise them. But it did entrance them.

"Girls! Peter Pan is back!" cooed the mermaid with a starfish on her dark locks.

A great amount of splashing and swishing caused a tumult of water worthy of a storm. More mermaids crowded around to see than before. At first they only had eyes for Peter, but they soon noticed the other boys and hissed at them, contorting their faces into disgust.

"Now, now, ladies of the water. Either you allow my friends to stay or I will not play my pipes for you."

Responses filled the air. "Oh no!" "They may stay — just flute for us!" "Oh very well." "Do keep them at a distance, though."

The one with a starfish on her locks said what many of the ladies were thinking. "Peter, you've changed." Indeed, he did not have as bright a countenance as last they saw him.

"I'm still the same me," he replied curtly.

"You're darling, Peter!" said the one with the shell sash, swimming up and pushing others aside.

"We adore you, Peter!"

"Ever so sweet!" said a third with red hair darker than Parx.

Peter Pan looked as if he didn't care about their compliments, but truthfully it did raise his spirits and for the first time since it happened he'd managed to not think about his poor goat. He grabbed his pipes and the music began.

Both the Lost Boys and the mermaids enjoyed his song, each stealing glances at the other now and then with the only difference being that the boys would like to get closer and the water ladies wished them further away.

Like his last visit, when Peter Pan finished he soared into the sky leaving them wanting more but not without collecting some of the adoration. He received cheers and a round of applause — both the normal way by hands and via tails slapping the sea. But Peter soon tired of it and went on his merry way.

The boys skimmed the tops of the trees, causing some of the fairies in their nests to shriek at them. But when they saw Pan in the lead they quickly changed to squeals of delight. Peter avoided passing by the Redskin camp, gnashing his pearly teeth in that direction. Darker and darker it grew, and the stars twinkled at him, as if guiding him to their next adventure. He flew up closer to them to ask if they had a destination in mind but they didn't have anything particularly interesting to say. He wanted someone to talk to other than the boys and the star-struck fairies of the island. He longed for home, thinking first of the Gardens and for a brief moment (in just the flicker of a star) his own bedroom window. But he called the Neverland home now. Could he not also consider Kensington Gardens home? Perhaps it is best to think of the Gardens now as a vacation spot. Vacating the Neverland seemed just what to do.

"Boys, I am making the journey back to the Gardens," Peter Pan announced, turning abruptly in flight. He quelled the round of joy by saying, "I shall go alone."

Rubadub squeaked out, "You don't mean to abandon us?" He looked more like a lost boy than ever.

Thinking of a certain window, Peter Pan cried out, "Never!"

"I am very glad. Are you glad, Parx?"

"Ever so glad. Are you glad, Jake?"

"Ay, I am glad. But Peter, when will you come back?"

"When I need to." His band did not appear at all satisfied with the answer. "Just always be waiting for me, and then one time you will find me back in our house under the ground." This reply contented them, anticipating the event already. "Jake, you play captain while I'm gone. And if you must get into trouble, be sure to get out of it." He dashed away. When his speck in the sky faded into the folds of the night, the Lost Boys were alone on the island and no longer felt very content.

Peter Pan followed the aerial trail around the world. He'd never traveled just by himself before, resulting in a twofold experience: a great sense of pride clung about him like his leaves and he fathomed a loneliness as deep as the oceans below. The long trip didn't appear any shorter, rather it seemed longer, but at any rate it he'd gone well into another twilight before he reached London. High enough that his former home looked like nothing more than a large green rectangle with darker green patches, sandy lines, a big blue spot and blue curve, he wondered how he could ever have lived in a place so small. To be fair, it is quite an expansive area. But not for those who can fly.

He wondered how he could ever have lived in a place so small

He landed atop a building across the street from Queens Gate and just as he set his feet down a clang sounded. Not just any clang but the very one heralding the Closing of the Gates. Peter Pan watched the people ambling out. Only Peter (and one little boy) saw the fairies shooing the people from behind, waving their hands with sour faces. Another *clang* from further off, then *clang, clang* a distance away. Peter Pan finally bore witness to Lock-out Time. How grand for him! A true new perspective on his old stomping grounds. Even grander, though, the sight of the children, both boys and girls, racing each other to the gates laughing all the way. To see real children at play! He remained out of sight, crouching and leaning with one leg bent and the other outstretched.

Another mysterious night in the Gardens sprang to life. From way up on the roof, Peter saw the three colors of lights dancing and dashing around as well as specks meandering across the fields. It reminded him of the Neverland, which jolted him into his reason for coming.

Without a care he leapt into the sky and descended on the other side of the locked gates. He purposely alighted away from any fairies for the moment, choosing instead to sit next to a blackbird. "Hullo," he said. "I've come back for a visit." The blackbird flapped a little, chirped as if annoyed, and with the chirp the loneliness of Peter's journey caught up to him. Pan didn't move, and he wanted to cry. But he did not. Instead he just sat still for a while, bemoaning the loss of the bird language, but when he considered what he had gained it did not seem such a bad trade. 'It is just as well,' he thought. 'For all they really chatter on about are their nests. If only they could use the leaves of the Neverland. What tiresome talks they would have about moistness and texture!' It still seemed unfair and scooting off the branch, he touched ground. He strolled the Broad Walk, wanting to catch the eye of a fairy and to see if he could be recognized. He received recognition to be sure, but in the form of awe, a deep fearful wonder, which is the very reason they did not swarm him.

"Peter?" said a voice.

The boy hoped he'd hear that particular voice. He whirled around and lifted into the air. "Ay, Colandrion. 'Tis me, Peter Pan." Did he will the sparkle in his eye or had it just shown up on its own?

"My lad! Sweet Grizel! Look at you!" He looped around Pan, scoping from all angles.

"Please don't say –"

"Wouldn't dream of it! Come, to Bird Island. It will be safer." Even though the walls surrounding the Gardens would shield him from view of the humans, he did not want to say that at his current size the boy might be spotted through the gates by a passerby.

Peter Pan flew after Colandrion, waving to all the fairies on both the ground and in the air as he went, relishing the attention. Yet at Peter Pan's request, he only had audience with Colandrion on the far side of the island. Firing up a whole fairy affair for his return ranked low on the list of what he wanted. He related to Colandrion as much of life in the Neverland as he could recall, which turned out to be a great deal more than the fairy expected to hear and Pan's adventures became known to him, more or less.

So as to delicately address how much Peter had grown, Colandrion landed on Pan's shoulder and said, "The Neverland can make each child's imagining real for them if they arrive. Perhaps the wish of *your* heart will seep into its shores as well."

"You mean not growing up?"

"If that is what you still want, Peter Pan."

Peter had forgotten about the very small old lady with the hooked nose altogether until now. "A little woman with a lot of long bumps on her face sort of like a tree told me the Neverland might already have that magic," he said happily. "Long before I reached its shores."

"Ah, then that is good for you."

He shifted his position and said, "I'm troubled I cannot talk to birds. Can you fairies return the language to me?"

"No," came the despondent answer.

"Oh."

Silence lingered for a while. Then came the tinkling of the darting mauve light, "Despite all the troubles you've had there, I want to see this crammed enchanted isle!"

"Come with me," Peter Pan said.

"If I can get permission from Mab."

"Why bother? She might say no. You're not a prisoner here," Peter said.

"By goodness! You are right, so let us leave."

"Not yet. I just arrived." A glaring oversight on Peter Pan's part, since he had in fact been talking to Colandrion long enough for a game of hide and seek amid the flowers to be fought over and won and a new 'it' selected. "Besides, I need to check for more boys."

A splash of grey formed into the darling underbite of Nickert. Peter Pan did not say so, but he could barely remember the rest of the Drowned Forest crew. The exact memories of it trickled and stretched as if looking through rippling water. But he'd no trouble recalling the little grey gargoyle fellow since he smiled with his adorable fangs right in front of him.

"Hullo," said Peter Pan.

"Why, Peter Pan! Just look at –"

"Stop right there," Pan commanded with his palm out and upright. "Yes, here I am, as I am, before you. Now," he said, switching topics like a fairy switches emotions, "who am I to take back and find a tree for?"

"If you mean boys, Pan, I regret to inform you that no more have fallen out of their prams. Nursemaids can be quite clever you know."

"Rot." He crossed his arms.

"And even if they had, Peter, it has not yet been seven days since you left."

"It hasn't?" he asked sincerely, noting how well the makeshift time of the island worked (or perhaps didn't).

"We'll have to work out a way to let you know when to come," Colandrion said.

"Can you tell me, though, if you please," said Nickert, wringing his hands, "about Jake? How is he doing? Does he show any…difference?"

"Funny you should ask," said Peter with a smile which quickly became a frown when he remembered what he must bring up to Nickert.

While Peter explained the trouble Jake had when he arrived at the island, the little imp played with his own tail and continued to twist and pat it some time after the boy stopped speaking. "Fascinating," he said. He began pacing. "I'd venture the other boys, not being their full selves, may slip through the film which obscures the Neverland, whereas Jake is a whole boy. So he finds it more difficult to get through."

"But I am more or less a whole boy, Nickert. Why can I break through with no trouble?"

"You are saturated in magic, Pan," Nickert explained. He zipped behind the lad and put little claws on his shoulders. "You may be a whole boy, but you are not a regular one."

"Pan's practically part bird, actually," said Colandrion.

Nickert whooshed back in front of the lad. "You are both broken via magic and fixed via magic, Peter Pan. The Neverland accommodates your kind, thus you can pass freely." He zipped away again and said while wringing his hands, "Tell me, the other boys, are they solid?"

"How do you mean?" asked Peter cocking his head and causing Colandrion to fly off.

"Are they just on the island in spirit or are they truly, actually, unequivocally there just the same as you and Jake?"

"That last part," replied Peter, though sure he didn't know what unequivocally meant.

"Fascinating," he repeated.

Pan asked, "What tried to keep out Jake?"

"I can only venture an inkling."

"How do I stop this inkling?" asked Peter.

He chuckled. "No, that's another word for a bit of an idea. Funny you should think the barrier is an inkling." He twisted his mouth up and down at the same time for a second or two, whooshing to a tree root and sitting down. "Many times on my travels I have noticed shadow-like figures. But they are not menacing. Rather like the opposite end of a night-light. Like eyes in the back of the head, sweetly watching." He picked up his tail and pet it gently. "I have seen them only a few times. But when I have, their force is one to be reckoned with, to be sure. A difficult, if not impossible, bond to break."

"Ah," said Colandrion, understanding before Peter Pan.

Nickert opened his big mouth again, but the fairy stayed him with motion of his hand. "Do not go on, please. It shall only enrage our dear Peter." He flew to the boy and used the same hand gesture. "Pan, since it will not alter the fact of its existence, leave some mystery for yourself, will you?"

Pan crossed his arms in a harrumph and turned his head upward and away to notice the glow of a throng of lights heading toward them. "Looks like word is out that I'm here," he sighed. Try as he may, he could not deny them their dance and blew a merry tune. But in the end his burning desire to have more fun with his band of adventurers, of course, won out. Peter Pan wished the fairies and critters a fond farewell, saying he'd be sure to return someday. Colandrion slipped away into the sky.

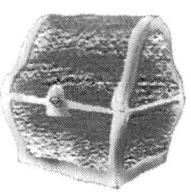

Chapter 12

Plans

Feeling confident that he knew the way, Peter flew alongside a pod of dolphins with no worry about venturing off course. He checked the stars and resumed the path in a wink. The fairy kept Peter in sight all the while, or at least most of the time, and caught up with him easily enough despite Pan's senseless wanderings.

Just when Colandrion doubted Peter knew the way, he saw the golden arrows pointing to Pan's home. Peter shielded his eyes from the sun which seemed to be staring right at him, piercing him with its shafts. He played at dropping like he didn't know how to fly, then eased his plummet to the speed of a lightly blowing leaf and hastened ahead.

Once again the fairy managed to keep Peter in view, though it proved much more difficult on account of all the wild wonders. Soon though, he followed right along into the Home Under the Ground. Colandrion looked upon it in peace as the Lost Boys were out at play. Like his wee folk kin, he gravitated toward the recess in the wall. He explored it for twice as long as he'd hovered around the big room. He might very well have gone on admiring it if not for the wild cheers. The Lost Boys must have come back, for who else could have made such a ruckus cheering Peter Pan's return? It seems a rather quick return, doesn't it? But not so for them, having amused themselves around the island for hours.

"Peter!" exclaimed Jake.

"Pan!" said Parx.

"Captain!" Rubadub saluted.

"Well, well, Peter," said Colandrion, shining into the center of the room. "It looks like you haven't exaggerated."

By now the Lost Boys had learned to decipher the tinkling of the fairy language.

"Who are you?" asked Rubadub with a smile.

"Mauve means which again?" asked Parx.

"Did you come with Peter from London?" asked Jake.

Flying to the face of each boy in succession, the fairy answered, "Colandrion, from the Court of Queen Mab. Boy. Indeed I did."

"He's visiting," said Peter uneventfully. He gave Parx and Rubadub an extra glance, but he couldn't place what struck him as different about them. "Well, tell me stories. What sort of mischief did you make?"

"We found a very small desert and came upon a jellyfish on the beach," said Parx.

"Is that all you could muster?" asked Pan in a mixture of disappointment and mockery.

"It seemed quiet, Peter," explained Jake.

"The whole island became lazy," said Rubadub, "like relaxing in a warm bath."

"But not so long ago the beasts snapped and clawed, the pirates prowled and we barely escaped from a band of trolls," Parx said.

"It all sprang to life," Jake said.

"Well, then, let's say hullo to it all!" Peter grabbed a sword and launched from his tree.

The Lost Boys took a deep breath and braced themselves for yet another run-in with danger. But at least now they had Peter Pan to lead the way and bail them out should they scrape too close to disaster. The wonderful boy pointed out sites of interest to Colandrion, especially those where he'd performed what in his mind counted as heroic deeds. After a rambunctious night, sleep ambushed them in their underground house.

Peter Pan awoke bright and early, glad to leave his nightmares behind. The other boys slept soundly, which is to say they made quite the sounds as they slept. Pan wondered if he'd been awakened by their snores, especially when he'd emerged from his tree and could still hear their gurgling beneath. Clearly something had to be done and Peter decided on the answer, so he ordered another round of work. He dropped back down his hollow tree and hovered over Rubadub. He kicked.

"OW!"

"Get up!" cried out Peter Pan.

"I say, what?" said Parx, rubbing fists into his big eyes.

"UP!" Pan shouted again. He then kicked Jake.

"Aye! I am up," he said, rubbing his rib.

"Where shall we explore today, captain Pan?" asked Parx.

"We're to do more work first."

"Ooo! May I carve out the mushroom?"

"No mushroom carving, Jake. You all wheeze like wild beasts when you sleep! We must muffle the sound with a barrier. We shall put doors on the entrances to our trees."

The boys did not seem as enthused as Pan.

Nevertheless, their lack of will did not prevent them from becoming little carpenters for the time being. Colandrion slept in the recess of the wall and did not rouse when Peter had wakened the boys. The fairy discovered them outside, hacking away at tree limbs. Although they looked ever so productive, the truth of the matter is they fiddled about with no real progress for none of them had any notion of how such a task is to be completed. It did not yet seem like work, since chopping and slashing can be ever so much fun. Colandrion asked Peter Pan about their activity and once Pan explained, the fairy said, "I can tell you how to manage it. I watched the Little House in Kensington Gardens go up a few times."

With Colandrion acting as their supervisor, tinkling orders here and jangling disapproves there, they managed to be rather productive. His first suggestion of bringing the smaller pieces of wood into the Underground House so as to work on the doors inside (since the boys had wondered how to fit a completed door down a tree) caused each boy to nod in assent to the correctness of the fairy's plan and they knew they'd made a good decision to put him in charge. Before long one of the doors had gone up, but quickly disassembled into a pile of planks.

"What's the matter with it?" asked Rubadub. "Do you know, Parx?"

"No, I cannot think what the matter is. Can you, Jake?"

"No, I cannot either. I pressed very hard on them together. Do you know, Peter?"

"No. Why don't they stay stuck?"

"Sweet Grizel!" cried Colandrion. "I suppose I shall have to lend you a helping hand." He sounded as if he scolded them for not realizing the error. Of course, he didn't bother to mention that they had not the tools like hammers, chisels and such of the fairies in the Gardens. But he also knew that perhaps didn't the little house had always been built with its fair share of magic assistance. So the fairy told them to line up the planks on the ground again. Rubadub made sure they were all just so until satisfied. Colandrion shook vigorously over the whole of the door, up and down the length of it. He regretted not bringing along a pouch of collected fairy dust as some of his kin had taken to doing once it became fashionable among all the best-dressed fairies. "Fairy fastening," he said. Sure enough, the planks became a proper door except for one detail. Alas, they had nothing to use as hinges and latches, so they merely leaned the doors against the tree holes. "Good enough," Peter decided. Taking a peek into the future for a brief moment, it can be seen that Pan procured the necessary components to attach the doors properly from pirate treasure chests.

Peter took over as supervisor since Colandrion handled the constructive duties. Of course, that only meant Pan watched them, lying on his side in midair, and shouting out quick and useless commands. The boys began to suspect that work might not be such a good idea after all.

While the rest of the doors they needed went up, Peter Pan finally put his finger on what had changed about two of his boys. As they worked, he could see that Parx and Rubadub were ever just that much taller than when they first arrived. Growing up! As soon as the thought struck Pan, he landed directly on the soles of his feet with a thud, thrust his dagger in their direction and said, "You have gotten bigger! You're not allowed to grow up! Stop it immediately or…," he fumbled, "or…I shall have to ensure that you don't, even if I have to whittle you down myself!"

Parx and Rubadub gulped, not wanting to ever see that look in Peter Pan's eyes again. Jake on the other hand breathed a sigh of relief as he had not grown even so much as another blonde lock of hair. Pan made a rapid exit, somehow able to slam one of the doors.

Colandrion went off in search of Peter and found him alighted in a nearby tree. It had not been difficult since Pan fluted to calm himself. The piping abruptly ceased.

"How can it be both ways?" wondered the wonderful boy.

"If you are speaking about the timelessness of the island," said the fairy, "obviously there's more going on than we are privy to, Peter."

Pan folded his arms, fidgeted with them, unfolded them, rested his elbows on the knees of his crossed legs and plopped his head on upturned fists. "We shall have to find her, Colandrion."

He needn't have asked who Pan meant. "Do you know where to look?"

"In the desert the Lost Boys found," he said. "It would seem I haven't explored that area enough, so that is where she must be."

Going by the boys' conflicting descriptions, Peter Pan eventually came upon a section of the Neverland tucked away in surrounding hills, almost as if the place did not wish to be found. He certainly did find the little desert, but wondered how the lads could have missed the palace hiding in the hills. Peter would have made a mad dash to the regal home but he had other concerns at the moment. He had all of forever to bother the royal residents. Right now he searched for the small old lady. He did not find her.

Just as he decided it to be a lost cause, a soft voice said, "Looking for me?"

Peter Pan turned around and there she stood. "I am."

Impressed with the grandeur of her years, Colandrion

surmised she must have been living protected in the castle. "Are you from the palace up yonder?"

"Me? In the palace? Dear no!" she giggled. "I have naught but a humble hut."

"Where is it?" Peter Pan asked.

"Never you mind that, boy. But do tell me what's on your mind."

Peter scratched his head, offended by her refusal to state the location of her home. But once again his current dilemmas won out. "You said the island will stop people from growing. But two of my boys have gotten bigger."

"Ah," said the woman with widening eyes. "But notice, Peter, that *you* have *not* for some time now."

He judged her statement by his leaves. They felt snug against him and not scratchy as they had on each occasion that he'd gotten bigger. "True," he said, quite pleased with the fact. "But how can it be both, lady?"

"I can only present evidence to you as it presents itself."

"You're no help at all!" snapped Peter.

The old woman sniffed outwardly with her hooked nose as if to brush aside the comment. Then she said, "You said two of your boys. What of the others?"

"There's only Jake. He has not grown either. But there is something even more curious about him."

"Oh?"

Once again, Peter Pan explained the trouble Higgins had in coming to the island. With Colandrion's help, he made sure to add in what Nickert had told them. The very small old lady with a hooked nose thought a long while, and Peter Pan nearly piped up to complain but the fairy stopped him, putting a wee hand on the boy's shoulder. Colandrion recognized a good think when he saw it.

"I, too, must agree with your friend," she said at last. She readied herself to speak again but the fairy raced over to her ear and whispered. "Ah," she said, taking his advice and not telling Peter Pan what she suspected. She didn't want a tantrum any more than the fairy.

"What are you whispering?" His eyebrows moved downward.

"Just giving her a bit of background on you, Peter."

"Oh."

The old lady said, "I can assure you of this, Peter Pan: You will always have the strength to fight these forces. Though it may not be to your advantage to do so. But it seems as if that is what you wish."

"It cannot hurt me or the boys who come?"

"It shall not hurt anyone, Pan."

"Never?"

"Never."

"I will always have the power to fight against it?" he asked with delight.

Her eyes narrowed. "Always," she agreed in a sigh.

Colandrion, of course, knew why the old lady sighed.

But Peter Pan did not in the least. In fact, he didn't even hear the exasperated sound for he'd been too preoccupied knowing how powerful he must be. To think that he could stand against the hostile force with no trouble at all! 'Tis a pity he didn't understand what caused it and an even greater pity that he now chose to give it no further thought.

The old lady turned up her hooked nose at the boy, spun around on her walking stick and disappeared into the woods. Likewise, Peter Pan disappeared into the sky, with Colandrion on his shoulder (as he'd become quite weary of trying to keep up.) The fairy expected him to move toward the palace but the truth is that Pan forgot about it entirely. But alas, Colandrion did not go all the way back to the Home Under the Ground.

Suddenly he slid from Peter's shoulder and plummeted. Pan noticed but thought the fairy mimicked his own playful action upon their arrival. Colandrion did not resume flight, delicately or otherwise. Not at all. Down he sank, like a hailstone. Peter Pan turned in midair and shot after his fairy friend. Soon he deemed it such a marvelous game that he too stopped flying and fell fast.

However, when Peter Pan reached the ground (hovering just before he crashed) he discovered that Colandrion had not been playing. Try as he might, he could not rouse the fairy. Then the awful truth hit Peter as if he had slammed into the ground. The whole way down, no mauve light had shone, just as no glow emanated from him now.

"NO!" Peter shouted.

A bunch of balls of light moved toward him. "Tisk, tisk, when will they learn?" cried a white one. "The horrid!" said another white. "What, again?" snided a blue one. "Oh dear," said a mauve. The rest just shook their wee little heads.

"Has what I think happened?" Peter asked with a sniff. He had been witness to it a handful of times before in Kensington Gardens.

"A child has become full of sense," came a blue reply.

"Some brat let loose the worst possible utterance known to fairies."

Peter Pan sniffed again. "It's not fair!" he yelled. "It's NOT FAIR!" he yelled harder.

"You're Peter Pan!" squealed a white light.

He didn't respond, rather annoyed that the death of his friend could be glossed over so easily, but he recalled that fairies could only feel one thing at a time. Perhaps they were to be envied. "It isn't fair," he muttered. "He'd been quite a good friend to me."

This statement sent some of the fairies flying away with upturned heads, jealous that one fairy could be prized over another by this magnificent boy. But some others consoled the boy saying, "You will always have plenty of fairies around you, Peter Pan."

"It isn't fair."

He jumped into the sky and try as they might these fairies could not keep pace with him.

He alighted on the jutting rock in Mermaids' Lagoon. Too busy singing, the water ladies did not see him at first. Peter listened to their gorgeous voices for a while but he couldn't last long not participating, so he accompanied them with a woodwind tune that both accented and fit with theirs. The mermaids stopped their song, for why bother themselves with singing when they could stare at the striking boy they adored? Peter Pan kept right on piping when their voices silenced. Note after note led into song after song and it became difficult to tell if it were not all the same tune. But it mattered little to the mermaids sighing in happiness. Their expressions turned sour when the Lost Boys flew down. The mermaids splashed water where the boys relaxed. They quickly disregarded each other, all too keen to be moved by the music.

None of them noticed the fizzling of the rainbows that stretched over the Lagoon like mystic foothills. Ever so gently their color faded and the arcs sagged. But Peter Pan's melody kept them all oblivious for most of the song. At a moment of rapid tooting, Parx looked up at the last sparkling trails of what used to be arched prisms.

"I say!" Parx said. "What's happened to the rainbows?"

Peter Pan stopped playing and looked over. "Rot." He'd come to the Lagoon to cheer himself. How terrible that its beauty should fade. What a nasty trick, he thought.

A sudden hissing noise grew loud, like one of the little waterfalls nearby had grown larger. Peter Pan pinpointed the real source with no trouble, but that is not to say that it hadn't been troubling. The mermaids themselves created the unpleasant sound. Their sheen dulled and they were no longer so lovely. Darkness had settled onto the island. Piteous moaning clung to the surroundings, clouding the very spirit of the place. Peter Pan would have flown away, so as not to have to put up with the unnerving sound, if he had not heard a voice.

"You think the Cap'n believes you *now*, Kempton?"

"What do I care? We's leaving tomorrow afternoon so the result's the same, innit?"

"We should bring the Cap'n out here. Just listen to this wailing!"

Either the bemoaned mermaid voices grew softer or the burly man voices grew louder, so Peter Pan plunked down to the other side of the stone on which he sat. The boys followed his lead. The splashes of water didn't alarm the buccaneers, who thought it merely the surf against the rocks.

Kempton laughed. "He won't bother himself to come this far off the ship. This be lackey work. And we's the lackeys."

"True," the other wavered.

Kempton laughed again, but in a mocking way. "You're afeared, ain't you?"

"Why couldn't we have come during the day?"

"Them ladies drown you fo' sure no matter t' time o' day."

No reply came other than splashes. A creaking noise followed by a clinking that continued on for a while. Peter Pan dared to creep up ever so slightly above the rock, just enough to see. The pirates hauled a small treasure chest, struggling to heave it into their dinghy. Kempton removed his blue bandana and wiped his brow with it. A heavy gust swept over the lagoon, and the bandana blew right out of his hands into a good floatation away. "Curses," he mumbled. The other pirate in a buckskin vest reached out to grab it. He leaned far in order to reach it and almost capsized the boat. "Watch out! Just leave it, Byford." And with that, Byford grabbed the oars and began pushing them across the water back toward their ship.

"Byford, it's *that* way," scolded Kempton.

"How can ye be sure in fog what clings t' the sea?"

"Byford, why do you always forget to navigate via stars?"

When he deemed it safe, Peter Pan crept up onto the rock and let out a call like a bird chirp. The Lost Boys flew up from the water. Peter flew out, nabbed the blue bandana and returned to his band by the rock. With a grin to be feared, he said, "I've a terrific idea." The Lost Boys gathered around and Pan whispered it to them, giving each of them specific instructions. They each nodded and then they dispersed.

Peter Pan flew back to the Home Under the Ground, popped through his tree and grabbed the great scimitar, still clutching the blue bandana and not touching ground all the while. Jake soundlessly soared after the pirates in the dinghy and

211

stayed on them as they climbed aboard the ship, keeping to the fog so as not to be seen but peering above it every now and then to keep abreast of the whereabouts of the small treasure chest. Parx and Rubadub moved onward to the Redskin camp, scoping out the number of and the positions of the vigilant braves.

They regrouped at a pool with a noisy waterfall. Peter Pan had the notion that the rushing water would drown out their voices in case anyone dare listen. After the boys gave their reports on their findings, Pan's wicked grin returned. It frightened Parx. "Tell me again why we're carrying out this plan?" While Parx posed his query to their captain, Rubadub took a moment or six to enjoy forceful scrubbing under the water current.

"I'm cross with them both," Pan answered. It did not seem enough for Parx, so Peter blurted out, "The Redskins killed my goat. And did you not see the pirates steal from the mermaids?" Parx now saw the reasoning behind the great plan, but he did not necessarily agree with Pan's logic. "Besides," Peter added, running his hand up and down the flat part of the scimitar, "the pirates think they can use the stars as a way to chart course as well. That's one of my tricks and they mustn't get away with it!" Upon hearing those words Parx questioned the reasoning that much more. But he also feared what Peter

Pan would do to him if he failed at his part to carry out the plan. Couldn't they lie out in a field and watch the night sky instead?

Jake and Rubadub, on the other hand, tingled with delight inside. What fun to not just be making mischief, but to be doing so with a design!

"Remember, Jake," said Peter. "Not too high up and not too far down. Or else they'll know it to be one of us."

"Aye, Captain Pan!"

They disbanded again, with Parx and Rubadub flying off one way and Peter Pan and Jake another. Under the watchful blinking stars they performed their tasks with ultimate stealth — always floating and making nary a noise. The only sound came from what could not be avoided when using a weapon and some animal imitations devised as an audible disguise. Peter Pan enjoyed mimicking the wild beasts.

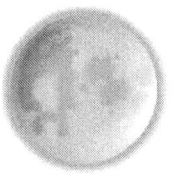

CHAPTER 13

EXECUTION

The boys did not return to the Underground House. If they had they would have missed all the ensuing shenanigans. What fun would it be to not see the reactions to what they had wrought? So they slept in shifts at a midway point from the Redskin camp and the pirate ship atop some palm trees. Fairies do not fancy living on the palm leaves as their little houses have a tendency to slide off, and despite their efforts to find a type of glue to stick them in place they found the adhesive lowered the whole character of the home. Thus, the boys did not have to contend with fluttering and angry tinklings as they gaily watched for signs of discontent.

When the sun had barely peeked over the island, Jake spotted the first action. Rumblings in the Redskin camp flared up. It began as shouting now and then, but it soon reached a constancy of yelling. By the severity and rapidity with which it came, the boys needed no translation. They only needed to understand the frustration to erupt into giggles and Pan laughed the most. When the Redskin encampment quieted, Peter and his band settled down. He ordered Rubadub and Parx to fly closer to the bay to better listen for an uproar from the pirates. He and Jake flew out toward the Redskin camp.

Pan wished he'd been able to see the moment the Redskins discovered the vandalism but he knew a closer proximity would not be wise. Yet from the branch on which they now stood, Peter could see just how well Jake had done his job. The scimitar jutted from the totem pole, its curve thrust deeply amid well placed hacks of defacement. Pan laughed again. One of the men held the still damp blue bandana.

"I hung it on the sword," assured Jake, "just like you said."

"Ripping!"

"How long before they go after the pirates for dishonoring their giant stick of faces?"

"I don't know, but it will not make a whit of difference. Should it take longer it shall only make the fun last all the longer."

215

Jake giggled. "The pirates might be on the prowl first, following the trail to their doom."

"I don't think them early risers like the Redskins. Yet they're due to set sail this afternoon, so perhaps they are up and about. And in their readying, they're just coming to find out what happened to their shiny and colorful things now."

Jake asked, "What happens when the Redskins and pirates come upon each other?"

"They fight tooth and nail, I suppose," said Pan.

Peter had in fact been correct about the pirates. As he spoke those words moments ago, Byford took note of the overturned chest. Not a single bauble, bracelet or coin glistened inside. Just painted feathers on the ground.

Parx and Rubadub delighted in hearing hollers once again. Unlike the Redskin voices, they understood the pirates' words not just because they knew the language, but from having flown close to the water. They hid behind a rock formation.

A louder, booming voice presided over the other manly moans, firing out like a continuous cannon. The boys realized it had to be the captain and looked at each other, sharing a hope that their own captain never barked at them the same way. The recent verbal thrashing and the point of a dagger still stuck in their minds.

Rile up buccaneers and they will buckle down quickly. A search party stirred up the sand before the boys could make sense of the nautical commands. They sauntered around the rock, keeping themselves out of view.

"Look! A gleam!" called one of the seafaring men. A jewel lay on the beach. "The blighters are careless!"

"What can you expect from a savage?" said another voice.

The boys watched the pirates slipping into the woods and then came another shout at finding a jewel. The voices died down and after a peek at the ship for a clear getaway, the boys moved into the sky following the path they knew the pirates were likely to trek on the treasure trail. "Looks like Peter Pan does know what he's doing," Rubadub said.

Indeed, their captain did have a handle on what would ensue from the mischief he had set into place. Surely he did not realize the whole of the outcome or he would not have been so keen on the plan in the first place. But for now it played out just as he wished.

The pirates decided on one of them forging ahead and the olive-skinned man named Torq won out by everyone's choice but his own. As he stomped over the undergrowth in sand-caked boots he calmed himself by patting the double-barreled flintlock pistol tied to his belt via a silk cord. Torq relished the advantage of another shot by way of its two triggers, especially since he could not claim a good aim among his best attributes. For that reason his baldric always held a cutlass at the ready.

Tall Ferret moved out on ahead for the Piccaninny Tribe with a large pouch strapped to his hip, next to a coil of withe and a tomahawk in his left hand. Tall Ferret took off without hesitation at the suggestion of a scout. He slinked along in a slow gait but used wide, sweeping steps to cover more ground. He kept alert, stopping to listen here or there and to place items in his pouch, but all the while crept steadily onward through the brushland.

Each would have come across the other sooner if either had moved more quickly instead of keeping a steady pace. Yet come face to face they did. Peter Pan and Jake watched the whole affair unfold under the thick branch on which they sat.

And what they saw happened like this: Tall Ferret showed no sign of surprise, raised his tomahawk high and rushed toward Torq. The pirate looked on in shock but for a moment before the double pistol pulled off a shot. Although he did not hit the man, he had disconnected the pouch at his side. It opened wide when it hit the ground, spilling forth a few doubloons and gems. The brave stopped in his tracks and regretted having picked them up along the way. "BILGE RAT!" yelled Torq, pulling the second trigger. Its speeding iron pellet would have torn a hole in the Redskin's chest had he not crouched some moments before to pick up a jewel. The pirate grunted and forcibly threw the pistol aside while whisking out his cutlass. In a fashion much like the tomahawk advance, he rushed at the native warrior. Tall Ferret, known for his wonderful aim, hurled the precious stone at Torq's hand. The burst of pain spread his fingers and down came the sword. Tall Ferret wasted no time whipping up the withe, curling it around the pirate's ankles and yanking hard, thus tripping the seaman into the land. In the graceful glide of his wide steps, the brave had picked up the pouch and stood over the pirate, brandishing the tomahawk. But he did not thrust it into him. He stuffed the pouch into the pirate's mouth to silence him and then quickly bound his legs. He used the tomahawk to obtain more withe from the forest and moved on to tying the fellow's arms at his side. Giving no regard to the man's comfort, Tall Ferret carried him to the tree and trussed him up against it.

    Peter Pan adored all of it, truly admiring the style of each fighter but his affinity leaned in favor of the Redskin since he used the world around him to help fight. Peter and Jake looked on, watching fear seep into the eyes of the pirate as the brave removed the flint from the pistol and in no time at all had a campfire blaze roaring. The Redskin grabbed a fallen branch of a pine and hacked at it with the tomahawk, riving it into splinters. He heated these chunks of wood in the fire and then came at the pirate with the red hot pokers. Unable to cry out, the man's eyes watered from the pain.

Peter Pan and Jake watched the whole affair

"Oh dear!" exclaimed Jake. He shot a glance at Peter Pan but could not make out his reaction to the horrid sight below.

The torture went on for a while longer until Tall Ferret let loose a howl in a rich deep tone that put the coyotes in the region to shame. Peter Pan narrowed his eyes at another trick of his being used, so he vowed to become better at imitation. The haunting melodic moan traveled to the ears of the Tribe who ventured toward it. Meanwhile, the buccaneers had begun to wonder why Torq did not return with news. So they tightened their grip on their weapons and embarked into the forests of the Neverland.

Not far behind flew Parx and Rubadub who sighted their friends on the tree. The long branch could accommodate them all. "The pirates are on their way," Parx reported. No sooner had he pointed at them just over yonder than a war-cry rang out, announcing the onslaught of the Redskins also headed their way.

"I'm ever so cunning," Peter Pan said with smile as an all out brouhaha sprang up below.

Like a magnetic pull, the two bands of men rushed toward each other. Spears, knives and swords clashed and already two have fallen. Byford threw a dirk at the withe to free Torq but to no avail. A brave ran him through just as some of the binding loosened and the pirate slumped to the ground. What a bloody brawl of buccaneers and braves!

Peter Pan's devilish grin might give one the idea that he enjoyed watching, but what proves even more telling is that he longed to join in the fight. Certainly the boy cannot have been expected to remain a spectator. With a mighty crow, the lad swung his arm out with his dagger upraised and landed gracefully amid the turmoil in the same way that children leap into two jump ropes moving in opposite directions.

The Lost Boys had to admit they craved more of the action below so they, too, eased their way into the battle, slashing as they came. For all their aerial antics, they may as well have been playing hopscotch and leap frog as well as jump rope. It's too bad the boys saw it as a game, for in a moment it would be so no longer!

Peter Pan flew around a Redskin and butted the dagger handle into his back, pushing him forward and down out of the way. This deft move gave Peter a great view of Jake holding his own against a pirate. But Jake lost ground in an instant and with a mighty thrust from his foe, he fell. Peter soared up out of harm's way to watch Jake get up. But Jake did not.

"NO!" cried out Pan, floating swiftly toward the pirate who had slain his friend. "NOT FAIR!" He could not believe it had happened. Despite one more hopeful glance, Jake still lay motionless on the ground. Peter Pan shredded the pirate. He stole the man's cutlass and hacked with double fisted weapons in a frenzy of flight into the thick of the fray. He wounded several of both types of men until he could no longer see from the water and sweat in his eyes. He darted into the sky entirely unscathed and swerved to avoid a hurled spear. He even managed to dodge an iron pellet.

By this time Parx and Rubadub came upon the awful truth about Jake. Parx suffered a deep cut the length of his thigh and Rubadub tired of fighting dirty. They joined their leader in the air.

Peter Pan gave one more pass over the scene, slicing at them all from the air, but he only could see Jake's ebbing blood. He dashed over the tree tops and did not stop his fast flying until safely on the other side of the island, if being close to a roving gang of wendigos could be counted as safe. The two boys remaining under his command caught up.

Rubadub said, "Jake –"

Peter Pan stared with the same intensity as before. Without speaking he conveyed that the topic must be dropped.

"May we go back to the hideout?" Parx dared to ask, pressing on his wound.

"If you wish it," said Peter coldly.

The boys needed no extra seconds to be on their way and even though they soon realized their captain did not follow behind them they kept on flying, all too anxious to be done with the awful game.

Peter meandered about and stepped into a shaft of moonlight. Bathed in the glow, he suddenly had an idea of how to rescue Jake. But he just could not, for any amount of trying, wrestle himself toward the other place. Though he could sense it, he could no longer go. It's just as well, for even if Jake were in sight, Pan had never brought a child back.

In a slow and sustained hovering Peter Pan leapt from oversized mushroom to branch to crag bounding about the island. But he could never escape from the death of his dearest friend. Worse still, he conjured up the demise of his other cherished playmates: his goat, the esteemed fairy Colandrion and even the memory of Old Solomon Caw plagued his mind. By the time Peter Pan had reached high atop the tallest mountain of the Neverland without using true flight so much as prolonged jumps, the moon hung low in the sky.

Chapter 14
Forever

Throughout most of the night, Peter Pan remained on the summit, having reached the peak of ire. He looked into the sky and the stars twinkled at him but they did not provide any comfort, as he had spited them for helping his enemies. Another vexation to entwine with agony. By the time the moon had fully risen, Peter Pan had crouched into a ball with his legs scrunched up against his chest and his arms wrapped tightly around them.

The magnificent isle sprawled out all around him below. The vast sea stretched on beyond the horizon. From this high up he could see all the seasons at once at various places but they switched with eerie ease when he looked again. His mind moved in much the same way. It zigged and zagged, a crazed terrain in desperate need of a mother to come and tidy it up. But alas, Peter Pan had given up all that came with a nursery. Instead of a room filled with toys, warm blankets and books on all topics, he had an island with weapons, strange foliage and creatures of all sorts. But in either case he still had an imagination. Should he go back? Surely he could fly home and see his mother, if only to sort out the mess he'd made stumbling around in the dark of his mind and the magical world. Would his mother even recognize him now that he'd gotten so big? He thought no. Decidedly no. Besides, she had her new boy and didn't need the likes of a wild son. Peter then heard laughter, a wicked laughter, but he soon recognized he'd made the sound himself and still chuckled on at the thought of that little boy. Just imagine! That son had no choice but to follow the path laid out for him in life. What a toad he must be — doomed to a life of discontent, caught in the mundane mainland daily routine.

  He smiled. He had escaped that horrid fate. And just as the fairies had intimated not so very long ago, he would always be surrounded by magic. But the smile did not last long when he recalled that he shared this place with petty fairies, murderous men and vicious beasts. Yet hadn't he been brought here for a purpose? Yes. To be the keeper of the island. To serve as a one-boy jury and justice in a place gone mad with magic and mayhem. He wondered if he could exist here in the Never-

Never Land if it meant a daily, nay hourly, regimen of risks which included losing those of whom he'd grown fond. Hadn't he felt like this many moons ago? Yes. When it came to pass that he didn't belong in the Kensington Gardens. But what other choice did he have? Either place — the magical or the ordinary — delivered its own set of the dreaded deeds thrust upon him, the ones known as responsibility.

A flash of Jake's lifeless form on the ground jolted into the maelstrom of his mind. Peter Pan saw the face of the pirate who slew his friend and then he saw that pirate lying on the ground dead. Killed by his own hand. The battle scene replayed in his mind.

'To think,' thought Peter Pan, 'those men came to this island.' And they showed up again from time to time, always coming back to this place, despite its tortures and perils. As did the Redskins, who remain. Surely, then, the island must be better than the real world at large. Pan thought, 'They chose to be here, or else the Neverland chose them. Just as it has chosen me.' He pulled himself up and counted himself among the lucky who could stand on the very island of imagination. But he didn't have to stand. He could soar above it all. "What a wonderful boy I am!" he said as he made his descent back down the mountain.

He managed to be a bit dancey, but halfway down Jake Mortimer Higgins crept back into his thoughts. "NO," said Peter Pan as he suddenly took to the air. He would not allow any of those pains to sour his mood. So he ever so sweetly whirled and skipped about, saying that nothing really means anything. He forced the thoughts and pains out like droves of people exiting at the *clang, clang* of the Closing of the Gates in Kensington Gardens. Lock-out Time had come at last.

He flew toward the ground and having thrown off his burdens, he suddenly felt so light so as to be pushed by a breeze. He kept a sharp eye out for activity in the dangerous and delightful playground. The Neverland — a wild Kensington Gardens, with gates that never closed and visitors coming and going in never-ending adventures.

Peter Pan now stood by a stream at the base of a hillock. The bark of a tree caught his eye and he tried to remember why he thought it special. But he could not recall and this frustrated him. Out came his dagger and he slashed at the tree. A sap oozed out. He focused on it for a while and then wiped his hand on it. He smeared the juices on the places that his suit of leaves showed some wear. He flew up to pluck skeleton leaves and used them as patches. He landed and felt truly himself. Why then did he stand frozen as if the cold of the London fog enveloped him? The chill broke from the hot stare of eyes above him. He gazed up at the very small old lady with the hooked nose at the top of the hillock.

"I know that look," she said.

"What look?" Peter asked looking rather befuddled.

"You may as well live in a wintered part of the island, boy."

"Go away," said Pan, starting to walk from her.

"I know what you've done," she called out.

The lad stopped, for just a moment, then continued slowly on his way across the ground.

"Your heart is cold," she said with fire in her voice. "It would behoove you to not keep it that way," she added as a friendly command, gripping her staff as tightly as Pan had hugged his knees.

"You can't tell me what to do, lady!" retorted the boy, turning around.

"But I can offer my advice. Allow the hurt. It stings, but you shall also heal, and from those experiences, grow."

Pan flew up at her in an instant. The nose of his youthful face nearly touched the hooked nose of her aged countenance. He sneered. "I will *never* grow up, do you understand?"

"Ay, I understand. Do *you*, boy?"

Peter Pan laughed, whooshing away from her, but slowed down a bit both in his flight and his chortling, thinking of the echoing dream laughter.

The old lady said, "The tragedy, my young friend, is that you shall get exactly what you want." She let the words sit in the air. Then she added just as ominously, "Don't count the days until you see me again. Most likely you shall forget you ever saw me at all."

"Well, good-bye," he said rather stand-offishly.

"And now, Peter Pan, I shall wait until then." She turned from him. "I shall wait until then," she trailed off, ambling away with her staff lifting and touching the ground in hypnotic rhythm. Soon the hillock blocked her from view.

Peter touched ground. How dare she! "Does she not know who I am? I am Peter Pan, the wonderful; the always a boy; master of the skies and Captain of the Neverland." He brought his pipes to his lips and began a merry tune.

He walked for a while and passed along a place not unlike a garden path. Swayed by his mystical music, flowers came moving after him in a long procession. Pan noticed the movement out of the corner of his eye, looked behind him, and could only say indignantly, "Look at those beastly flowers following me." He signed to the flowers authoritatively to stop it. They stood still. He resumed his pipes, satisfied that he'd been obeyed. He went on and disappeared around an enormous shrub with points like a crown. The flowers began to trail him again, but Pan had only been hiding. He popped around the shrubbery and caught them following. Again they stopped. Peter waved to them to go back from whence they came and so they all moved along until there were none left, behaving precisely in the manner of a dog chasing its master and then ordered home. Peter Pan nodded with smug conviction and flew into the sky.

Flowers came moving after him in a long procession.

As he flew the odd incident of the floral followers stuck with him. A rather curious instance of magic indeed and it set his mind to racing about his own magical nature. What a marvelous life he'd led so far! Why, then, could he not remember much of it? Did it matter, he wondered? He knew what he needed to recall, more or less. He knew his mother had replaced him with another son. That he'd flown away to Kensington Gardens. So what if he could no longer properly converse with the birds as he used to, or be literate as he once had been? He could still understand the fairy language and play Nature itself on his pipes. He'd always have new friends. Yet he did not recall exactly why, except that he could fetch more back in the Gardens. For you see, like the two boys now with him on the island, he no longer remembered the Drowned Forest. But no tears must be shed. Those in the Drowned Forest are quite used to being forgotten, so another bout with oblivion would not faze them any more than dispersing a reflection in a pond by skipping a stone. And yet, much of their teachings still showed up in his mind. "I can only remember things here and there," Peter Pan told himself, "so I may as well make up the rest."

He could no longer wrestle out his spirit to follow those children part of the way beyond. But he had something much better. He'd become the very spirit of youth.

Indeed, it must be so, for he now felt as light as a spirit. The proverbial song in his heart, he landed at the entrance to his grand home beneath the surface. Standing alongside the hollow trees, gateways to above and below, he played another round on his pipes. And something occurred to him. Something rather telling. Such mystical music came from naught but mere bound reeds. The pipes existed right on the cusp of the earthen and the ethereal. He, too, existed right on the cusp: Natural and otherworldly. Infant and grown-up. Novice and master. Life and death. The mainland and the Neverland. Dreams and reality. Peter Pan grinned in a sigh. Everything seemed right with his world. "I still *am* the Betwixt-and-Between!"

Escapades came and went, and some of them proved more notable than others. Take for instance the exploration of the palace hidden amid the foothills, or the shenanigans at the shallow pond that only has fish when the sun is half past the bush shaped like an egg, or the time Peter Pan stole a pirate dinghy and sailed around the ocean for a while and met up with a very menacing creature. And so it goes — one adventure after the next. At this time four boys serve under Peter Pan on the marvelous island known as the Neverland. One shall meet his demise this very evening, but another is always on the way.

Made in the USA
Charleston, SC
16 March 2013